THE
CHRISTMAS ANGEL PROJECT

Books by Melody Carlson

Christmas at Harrington's
The Christmas Bus
The Christmas Shoppe
The Joy of Christmas
The Treasure of Christmas
The Christmas Pony
A Simple Christmas Wish
The Christmas Cat
The Christmas Joy Ride
The Christmas Angel Project

THE

CHRISTMAS
ANGEL
PROJECT

MELODY
CARLSON

Revell

a division of Baker Publishing Group
Grand Rapids, Michigan

Published by Revell
a division of Baker Publishing Group
PO Box 6287, Grand Rapids, MI 49516-6287
www.revellbooks.com

Printed in the United States of America

Library of Congress Cataloging-in-Publication Data
Names: Carlson, Melody, author.
Title: The Christmas angel project / Melody Carlson.
Description: Grand Rapids, MI : Revell, a division of Baker Publishing Group,
    [2016]
Identifiers: LCCN 2016011145 | ISBN 9780800722692 (hardcover)
Subjects: LCSH: Life change events—Fiction. | Generosity—Fiction. | Charity—
    Fiction. | Christmas stories. | GSAFD: Christian fiction.
Classification: LCC PS3553.A73257 C455 2016 | DDC 813/.54—dc23
LC record available at https://lccn.loc.gov/2016011145

In keeping with biblical principles of creation stewardship, Baker Publishing Group advocates the responsible use of our natural resources. As a member of the Green Press Initiative, our company uses recycled paper when possible. The text paper of this book is composed in part of post-consumer waste.

16 17 18 19 20 21 22   7 6 5 4 3 2 1

Prologue

Abby Wentworth sighed with contentment as she leaned into the soft plush sofa. "I think this was the best Thanksgiving ever." She smiled happily as her husband set another log on the already crackling fire. "I mean, despite not having any of our family members with us this year, it went really well. Don't you think so too?"

"I'll say." Clayton chuckled as he closed the fireplace door. "In fact, that's probably why it was so pleasant—no family feuds or old emotional fires to put out." He brushed off his hands, then sat down next to her. "I'm well aware of how difficult some of my siblings can be during the holidays. Remember how Edith and Dorrie bickered over the cranberry sauce last year?"

"That's right! Homemade versus store-bought—I almost had to hide the turkey carving knife." She laughed.

"No drama like that today."

"But I must admit that Grace and Joel seemed a little strained—although they hid it well. Did you notice?"

"Yeah, but I chalked it up to having young adult kids." Clayton slipped his arm around her shoulders, snuggling her closer to him. "The twins seemed like they were in a snit, like they couldn't wait to get away from their parents."

"I'll bet that's why Grace asked me to meet her for coffee on Saturday."

"My little Abby Angel—the constant counselor." Clayton gave her a squeeze. "What would your book group friends do without you?"

"You know that they're more than just *book group* friends," she reminded him. "Furthermore, what would *I* do without them? Those girlfriends have gotten me through a lot, Clayton."

"Believe me, I know." He leaned over to peck her on the cheek. "And I'm very grateful for them, Abby. I really am."

She picked up her sewing basket from the coffee table, setting it on her lap as she opened the lid. "That's how I've been feeling lately too. Very thankful for all four of them." She removed one of the four Christmas ornaments that she'd been working on this past week. "That's why I made these."

He studied the ornament hanging from her finger. "I'm married to such a clever woman." He gave it a twirl. "They'll love these, Abs."

"This is the last one. For Louisa." She took out a needle and spool of white thread. "It's nearly done. I think I'll finish it up tonight."

"Just so you know, I'm on KP. If I see you step one toe in the kitchen, you're toast. You hear?"

"Thanks, hon." She grinned as she put on her reading glasses. "Wouldn't want to be toast . . . although I would like a cup of freshly brewed decaf. But it's hard to make any if I can't get into my kitchen."

"One cup of decaf coming up." He gave her a mock salute. "How about a little pumpkin pie to go with it?"

She laughed. "And here I thought I'd never be hungry again. Yes, please! Bring on the pie and coffee."

As Clayton headed for the kitchen, Abby started to hum softly to herself. One of her favorite Christmas carols—and perfect for her sewing project. Before long she was singing the words aloud:

> Hark the herald angels sing,
> "Glory to the newborn king!
> Peace on earth and mercy mild,
> God and sinners reconciled."
>
> Joyful all ye nations rise,
> Join the triumph of the skies,
> With angelic host proclaim,
> Christ is born in Bethlehem!

1

Belinda Michaels was shocked to hear the news: her best friend, Abby Wentworth, had passed away in her sleep. According to Abby's husband, who called shortly after 6:00 a.m., Abby had gone to bed with a severe headache last night, the day after Thanksgiving.

"It's too early to say, but the medical examiner suspects an aneurism." Clayton spoke in a hoarse whisper that was almost unrecognizable. "I already called her dad . . . and the principal at her school . . . and now you."

Belinda was so shocked that she could barely form words, but she somehow managed to express her sincere condolences to Clayton. "If there's anything I can do—" Her voice cracked with emotion. "Please—feel free to ask."

"Just let the other book group friends know," he said sadly. "You women meant the world to her." Belinda promised to do so, telling Clayton that he'd be in her prayers. But as soon as she set down her phone, she fell completely apart. After a long, hard cry, her sadness turned to anger and she began storming through her house. Ranting and raving, she shook her fist at the ceiling.

Why would God take Abby when she was only in her forties and the world still needed her? Abby had been a perennial optimist, loyal friend, beloved kindergarten teacher, and generally wonderful person. Why would God take her like that? Especially after Abby had fought and won her battle against ovarian cancer. Just two days ago, at their Thanksgiving get-together, they'd toasted to her six years of remission. And now she was dead from a brain aneurism? How could that be? How was that fair? And what would Belinda do without her?

Belinda finally found herself standing in front of her stone fireplace, just shaking her head. On the solid oak mantle were several framed photos. Mostly of her daughter Emma at various ages—from birth to her twentieth birthday last spring. But it was the old black-and-white photo, taken back in the thirties when Belinda's mother had been a toddler, that caught Belinda's attention now. Her round-faced mother had been seated on her great-grandma's lap. Belinda had known since childhood that the wrinkled old woman, simply known as Granny, had been born into slavery. "She's why we got to be strong," Belinda's mother used to tell her as a child. "We gotta make Granny proud."

Attempting to steady herself and be strong, Belinda took in a deep breath as she looked at the clock next to the old photo. Surprised to see that it was nearly 7:00 now, she knew it was time to call the other book group friends. Louisa and Grace and Cassidy needed to hear the news. But how do you say something like this? Talk about a bad wake-up call.

Knowing that Louisa Van Horn was Abby's oldest friend and mentor, as well as an early riser, Belinda decided to start with her. She quickly blurted out what Clayton had told her.

Not surprisingly, the older woman broke into soft sobs, each one wrenching through Belinda's already hurting heart. Louisa was barely over losing her husband last winter—and now this.

"I can't believe it," Louisa declared in a husky voice. "Our sweet Abby is gone? How can that be?"

Belinda shared what little information Clayton had given her and then, in an attempt to end the painful conversation, she explained that she still needed to call Grace and Cassidy.

"I think we should all meet," Louisa said suddenly. "Abby would want us to be together right now." They agreed to meet at the Coffee Cup later in the day. Belinda told Louisa goodbye, then prepared herself to call Grace.

As she waited for Grace to answer, Belinda wished that she felt closer to this woman. It bothered her to remember how she'd sometimes been jealous of Grace—often worried that Grace was trying to steal Abby's friendship from her. Not that it had ever happened. Now she felt guilty for her juvenile feelings. Grace answered her phone in a sleepy voice and Belinda quickly told her the distressing news, followed by Louisa's suggestion that they meet later in the day. Then she tried to cut the conversation short by explaining that she still needed to call Cassidy.

"Poor Cass," Grace said. "Abby was like a mom to her."

"I know." Belinda winced to think of how Cassidy would take this. It would be the most difficult phone call to make.

"I feel so lost now." Grace sniffed loudly. "I can't believe I can't just text her—can't believe Abby's really gone."

Belinda attempted to say words of comfort, but knew they sounded as stiff as a poorly written sympathy card. "I better call Cass," she finally said. "I promised Clayton I would let everyone know."

"I'll see you this afternoon," Grace said.

Belinda told her goodbye, then pushed the speed dial for

Cassidy's number, taking in a deep breath as she waited for the young woman to answer. Since it was Saturday, it was possible that she'd already be at the veterinary clinic. She'd probably have her phone in her pocket to check texts, but Belinda didn't want to text her with this kind of news.

"Hey, Bee," Cassidy said cheerfully. "What's up?"

Belinda quickly broke the news about Abby, but when Cassidy didn't respond, Belinda thought maybe she'd lost the connection. "Cassidy?" she said loudly. "You still there?"

"Yeah—I'm here—I—" Cassidy's voice broke. "I don't know what to say. I can't believe it. How can she be dead? We just saw her on Thanksgiving. She was perfectly fine."

"I know, honey."

"I feel like I can't breathe."

"Sit down and take some deep breaths," Belinda said slowly.

"Abby was—was like a mom to me. I mean, she wasn't old enough, but you know what I mean."

"I know, Cass. She loved you so much. She was so proud of what you've made of your life."

"What will I do without her?"

"You've still got me," Belinda said meekly, although she knew that she could never replace Abby—no one could. "And you've got Louisa and Grace too." Now she told Cassidy about Louisa's suggestion. "Three o'clock at the Coffee Cup—can you make it?"

"Yeah, I get off work at two."

"Maybe they'll let you have the day off. I mean, considering—"

"No, I'm the only vet here until Dr. Auberon comes in at two."

"Well, go easy on yourself, honey. Take lots of deep breaths. And remember how much Abby loved you."

"Yeah—it's just that—that I will miss her . . . so much. I don't know what I'll do without her."

"We'll figure it out," Belinda assured her.

By the time Belinda hung up the phone, she felt like a dishrag that had been completely twisted and wrung out—thoroughly drained. And she still felt miffed at God. Didn't he know how many lives would be devastated by Abby Wentworth's death? Not only her family and close friends either. All of Lincoln Elementary would feel the loss.

For that matter, many of the residents of Pine Grove, Minnesota, would feel it as well. And just before Christmas too. How could any of them expect to have a good Christmas now?

2

Even though Louisa was the oldest member of the book group, Abby had always been the leader—the glue that held them together. In fact, she'd been the one to start the book group in the first place, more than fifteen years ago. Originally they'd had eight members, but it didn't take long before they were whittled down to just five. And that, they'd decided, was how they wanted to keep it. But now there were only four.

Louisa glanced at her watch as she went into the Coffee Cup. She was a few minutes early, but that would give her a chance to order her latte and get them a table. To her surprise, the big table in the corner was free. As she carried her latte back there she remembered the first time they'd met as a book group—at that very table. She also remembered the time they'd met there about nine years ago when Abby had told them she had ovarian cancer. Louisa sighed as she sat down. And now Abby was gone.

As Louisa picked up her coffee, she noticed her hand—surprised to see how old and wrinkled it looked, with blue veins showing through her pale skin. She'd turned sixty-three in April, shortly after Adam passed away. If any of the book group women needed to die, it should've been her. Widowed and lonely, Louisa had been attempting to hide her struggles with depression this fall. Just a few days ago, she'd confessed to Abby how she was not looking forward to Christmas this year. "Matthew and Leah and the kids can't come home from Dubai—and I told them not to worry about it," she'd confided. "It's so far for them to travel and, really, it's just one day. Maybe I'll just forget about Christmas altogether."

"Well, you will be spending Christmas with Clayton and me," Abby had declared. "And we'll invite some others too. Maybe the book group would like to get together again—like we did last year. That was fun playing games like we did."

Louisa sighed sadly as she sipped her latte. And now Abby was gone. Christmas would be bleak this year. As she set down her cup, she noticed Grace coming through the door. With her shoulder-length auburn hair, creamy skin, and sparkling turquoise eyes, the successful designer was hard to miss—and she was always stylishly dressed. Today Grace had on a rust-colored suede jacket, dark pants, and a colorful scarf—put together as usual, except that she looked very gloomy.

Louisa made a sad little wave as Grace went to the counter to order her coffee. Grace waved back, but her usual smile was absent. Louisa made an involuntary shiver, and although it wasn't cool in here, she pulled her plaid shawl more snugly around her shoulders. Maybe this idea of hers, to get the book group together, wasn't such a smart plan. Everyone would be so blue. What good could come of it?

Now she observed Belinda coming in. As usual, Belinda looked chic too. Even when she just threw something on, like she'd probably done today with her worn and torn jeans and black leather jacket, she wound up looking like something from a fashion magazine. Being tall and thin helped, but beyond that Belinda was just plain beautiful. Of course, Belinda didn't see herself like that, but that was just part of her charm. Today, despite her dark glasses, which she kept on even though she was inside, and her chestnut-brown hair stuffed into a tweed fedora, the woman still looked stunning. Louisa looked down at her latte, noticing not for the first time how it was almost the same shade as Belinda's complexion. Louisa had asked to paint Belinda's portrait several times, but Belinda always just laughed about it. Since Adam's death, Louisa rarely picked up a paintbrush anyway. And at the moment, she couldn't imagine tackling a blank canvas. She would rather undergo a root canal.

Belinda and Grace were talking at the counter, and to Louisa's surprise they actually embraced. That was something Louisa had never witnessed before—and it would've made Abby happy. Louisa had sometimes wondered if those two were in competition for Abby's friendship. Belinda and Abby had been best friends for decades, and Grace was the relative newcomer. But Louisa knew that Belinda could be insecure at times.

The last one to show up was Cassidy. She came into the coffee shop just as Grace and Belinda were picking up their coffees. Still wearing her drab veterinary work clothes, Cassidy appeared tense and tired. Her honey-blonde hair was pulled back in a ponytail and, even from a distance, Louisa could see from her pale blue eyes that she'd been crying quite recently. Louisa's heart went out to the poor girl. Oh, Louisa knew that Cass wasn't really a girl. Despite the fact she could easily pass for being in her early twenties, Cassidy would turn thirty-five in January. And to hear Cass go on about her "spinsterhood," one would think she was Louisa's age.

Louisa stood up as Grace and Belinda approached. Waiting for them to set down their coffees, she hugged them both.

Before long, Cassidy came over and all four joined together in a group hug, complete with more tears.

"I'm numb," Belinda said as she sat down. "I still can't believe it."

"I know what you mean. I keep thinking of how Abby was so full of life," Grace added. "She could light up a room just by entering it."

"Even when she was doing chemo," Cassidy said sadly. "Remember how the nurses were always so happy to see her? She'd get the whole place laughing in no time."

"And what about the students in her classroom?" Belinda grimly shook her head. "They'll be devastated when they hear the news."

"I hadn't even thought about that." Cassidy's eyes glistened with tears. "It's just so wrong."

"It seems impossible that she's gone." Grace sighed.

"I feel so confused." Cassidy blotted her tears with a napkin. "I was relieved that the vet clinic was slow today. I don't know what I would've done if I'd had to deal with an emergency or an intense procedure."

Louisa patted Cassidy's shoulder. Suddenly, since she'd suggested this impromptu meeting, she felt responsible for everyone's gloominess. "I know that we're all very sad," she said slowly, "but I'd hoped that we could encourage each other today." She frowned. "It's just that I don't even know how to do that right now."

"I wonder how Clayton is doing." Grace looked at Belinda. "How did he sound?"

"Like he's barely holding on."

"I talked to him a little bit ago," Louisa told them. "I asked if we could drop off some food or something. But he said it was just him at the house and that he had no appetite. Besides that, he said someone from his church had already brought a casserole." She shook her head. "He'll probably be buried in food before long. That's what happened to me when Adam passed away."

"Guess that's why they call it comfort food," Belinda said wryly.

"Clayton asked me to inform you that the memorial is scheduled for Tuesday at ten thirty," Louisa said. "He said that Pastor Gregg will invite people to share memories of Abby, and he's hoping we'll all speak up."

For a while they discussed what they might say during the memorial service and ways they could help Clayton during this difficult time. It seemed to distract them from their own personal sadness for a bit, but Louisa could tell that they were all still suffering. Finally, unsure how much more she could take, Louisa began to get fidgety.

"I should probably get going," she said abruptly, trying to think of some sort of believable excuse for leaving so soon. In reality she was on the verge of more tears, and she just didn't want to chance falling apart all over again. Really, what good would that do?

"Me too." Cassidy stood. "Lulu and Bess are probably missing me by now."

"Tell the kitties hello," Louisa said meekly as she fumbled to gather her purse and gloves.

Belinda and Grace stood at the same time, both saying they needed to go check on their businesses—although Louisa knew that neither of them usually worked on Saturdays, and she doubted they would be working today. But despite her suspicions that they were all going home to have another good cry, she didn't say a word. Quite honestly, she didn't know how to prevent it. Besides, she knew from what she'd gone through since losing Adam, grief must run its course. Sometimes that course could be long and lonely.

Outside of the Coffee Cup, they all shared another group hug, promised to keep in touch, and then parted ways. As Louisa got into her old BMW, she wondered just how well they would stay in touch now that Abby was gone. She didn't think she had the energy. Just driving home felt exhausting to her.

Louisa was so tired that she felt like she could sleep for about a year as she turned into her gated neighborhood. She remembered how happy she'd been when she and Adam had bought a house in the Grove. According to Grace's husband, their optimistic Realtor, the Grove was the swankiest neighborhood in town. "You can't go wrong investing here," he'd assured them. But they'd barely unpacked when the economy took a dive that ultimately dissolved their substantial down payment. As a result, Adam had told her they would probably have to spend the rest of their days there. As it turned out, he did. She probably would as well.

As she drove into the garage, she thought once again how this house was too big for her. When they were in their fifties, it had seemed just right. Her only child, Matthew, and his wife were just starting their family, and Louisa had dreamed of hosting delightful Christmases and other holidays surrounded by her loved ones. But several years ago, Matthew's job had relocated them to Dubai, of all places. Although he'd made it home for his father's funeral, he didn't expect to bring the family back again for at least another year . . . maybe two.

Matthew had been encouraging Louisa to come visit them, but the idea of traveling halfway around the globe on her own was overwhelming at best. So much so that Abby had offered to be her traveling companion. Remembering this, and realizing it would never happen now, Louisa's heart grew even heavier as she went into the house. And when she saw the box of Christmas decorations—still in the laundry room where she'd set them only yesterday—her eyes filled with tears. She'd gotten them out, thanks to Abby's encouragement—determined to make her home festive. "Fake it until you make it," Abby had cheerfully told Louisa on Thanksgiving. "Decorate your house for Christmas and you'll start to feel the Christmas spirit."

Louisa carried the box out to the garage and shoved it back into the cabinet where it belonged. Slamming the cabinet door shut, she burst into tears.

Although Grace had already told her assistant, Camille, that she didn't plan to return to work after Abby's memorial service, she found herself sneaking in the back door and tiptoeing through the design showroom just the same. She slipped up the back stairway that led to her studio loft on the second floor and there, despite her cheerful bravado at the memorial service, Grace couldn't hold back the tears.

The truth was, her outburst was only partly related to Abby. The rest of the unbridled emotion came from frustration over a lot of things. Her marriage, her kids, even her career—none of it seemed to be on track. Not the way she had expected, anyway. Only this morning, she and her husband, Joel, had gotten into an argument over the twins. Lauren and Hunter were both in their second year of college, and neither was doing well. According to Lauren, Hunter was drinking and partying at school—even more so than last year. As a result, his grades were probably in the toilet. According to Hunter, Lauren was doing the exact same thing.

Grace and Joel had attempted to express their concerns to them during the past weekend when the twins came home for Thanksgiving, but thanks to Joel's lack of volume control, the discussion had quickly degenerated into a shouting match. Now that the twins were back at school, Grace felt even more worried about them. Underage drinking and the dangers associated with it were enough to distress a parent, and Joel wasn't helping.

This morning, on their way to the memorial service, Joel had gotten on his high horse over the wasted tuition money. Although Grace didn't appreciate his ill-timed temper tantrum, she couldn't really blame him. Tuition for the twins was a considerable amount of cash, everything they had worked to scrimp and save during the past twenty years.

Grace blamed Joel for the fact that Lauren and Hunter had seemed to join forces against their parents this past weekend. It was as if the two nineteen-year-olds had simultaneously decided to stop listening to them. As if they had forgotten that they were completely dependent on parental financial support, certain that they should be able to call the shots in their own lives. The two had been downright belligerent.

Naturally, she and Joel had been aggravated—and just as naturally, they could not agree on any sort of solution. Frustrated by Joel's outbursts, Grace had planned to meet with Abby on Saturday for some helpful advice and encouragement. Abby, though childless, had always been one of the best counselors when it came to child rearing. Grace wasn't sure what she would've done without Abby these past fifteen years.

But now Abby was gone. And Grace, like a rudderless ship in swirling seas, felt desperate. Joel seemed to be adopting a "let them sink or swim" attitude. As if it made no difference if the twins never finished their education. Was the man nuts? Or was he simply making her nuts?

"*Grace?*" Camille froze in the doorway with a surprised expression. "I'm so sorry—I didn't realize you were up here. I needed the Spangler file. Val Spangler is downstairs looking at upholstery fabrics and—"

"It's right here." Grace started fumbling through the stacks on her oversized desk, wiping her tear-streaked cheeks with her other hand.

"Are you okay?" Camille came closer, curiously peering down at her.

"Yes, I'm fine." Grace snatched up the thick file.

"I thought you weren't coming in after the service."

"I had some drawings to work on."

"Want me to take that to Val?" Camille reached for it.

"No." Grace stood with the file held close to her chest. "I'll talk to Val. Thank you."

Camille backed off as if offended.

Grace forced a stiff smile, knowing she'd spoken harshly. "Sorry, Camille. But I think I'd feel better being busy. You know?"

"Sure." Camille nodded but looked doubtful, as if she wanted some kind of explanation, which Grace was determined not to give. Camille was a fairly hard worker, but she could be slightly intrusive at times. Sometimes it felt like she wanted to step into Grace's shoes—for instance, with Val Spangler right now. Didn't she know how difficult Val could be? Did Camille honestly think she could handle that? But a challenging client was exactly what Grace needed right now—something to block out the other complicated areas of her life . . . so many things that she couldn't control. At least she ought to be able to control Val.

Belinda felt confused and depressed as she walked through town after the memorial service. At first she thought she was going home, but the idea of being alone right now was not appealing. She didn't need to go ranting through her house again. Or crying uncontrollably.

So she turned back toward town, deciding it was a good time to get started on creating a new window display at her thrift store. She never actually called Glad Rags a *thrift store*, per se. Long ago, she'd learned to use more appealing terms like *resale* or *recycled*, or the recent catchphrase *up-cycled*. And since most of the carefully selected and "gently" used items were refurbished and refashioned, they were, in a sense, even better than new. In fact, most of them wound up being unique, one-of-a-kind items—something her clientele, mostly twenty-somethings, appreciated. Providing quality merchandise was what had supported her and Emma for years. Ever since Byron Michaels had left them, back when baby Emma was still in diapers. Belinda had felt hurt and rejected by the abandonment for years, but she knew that Byron had broken a string of hearts after hers. According to Emma, who stayed loosely in touch with her father, Byron planned to wed his seventh wife before the New Year.

Fortunately, Belinda had moved on long ago. With her mother's help, she'd leased a nice shop and started a resale business with children's clothing and merchandise. Running her own shop had been compatible with raising a young child since Belinda could bring Emma to work with her. As Emma matured, so did the business—until it finally morphed into the chic resale boutique that it was today. A place where Emma and her stylish friends still loved to shop.

But this wasn't what occupied her thoughts as she started to arrange various items of clothing and accessories in the store's front window. Her troubled mind was on Abby and the service she'd just attended. All in all, it had been a truly lovely service. There were no doubts that Abby had been well loved by everyone fortunate enough to cross her path. Belinda knew she was very lucky to have been considered Abby's best friend all these years. No, not lucky. As her mom would say, Belinda was *blessed*.

The general consensus at the service today was that Abby would be warmly welcomed in heaven. No doubts about that. Abby had never "hidden her light under a bushel." In fact, as Pastor Gregg had said, Abby's entire life had been like a bright beacon of pure golden light. Abby had never been one to verbally preach about God, but she didn't need to. Abby had lived out God's love and goodness, spreading it among friends, co-workers, students, gas station attendants, grocery store clerks, lost puppy dogs. The memorial service had been packed with people who'd been touched by Abby. It had been a true celebration of life—and justly so, because Abby was worth celebrating.

Belinda tried a glitzy belt around the black dress she was toying with, then tossed it aside. Her problem today was not really about Abby. It was with God. Why did God think Abby would be more useful in heaven than down here? Didn't heaven have enough wonderful people in it? Why take Abby? It made no sense. And the more Belinda thought about it, the more frustrated she became.

Her attempt to distract herself was not working! At times like this, Belinda really wanted to talk to someone. Someone like Abby. When Abby was unavailable, Belinda's mother would be her choice . . . but she had passed away several years ago. And her grandmother might've been helpful, except that she now suffered from dementia. There was no way she wanted to burden Emma with this. Emma had already been distraught over Abby's death, not to mention bummed over not being able to attend the service because of finals.

Belinda gave up on the display, heaping the items she'd collected on the counter and instructing Savannah, her sales clerk, to put them away when she wasn't busy.

"It was a mistake for me to try to work today," she told Savannah as she retrieved her bag from beneath the counter. "I'm going home."

"Sorry you're still feeling bad," Savannah said, "but you probably need to give yourself time."

"Time?" Belinda looked blankly at her young employee.

"You know, to grieve. It's what the books say to do."

Belinda rolled her eyes. "Yeah, you're probably right. See you tomorrow." As she headed back out to the street, she felt another wave of sadness washing over her—almost as if she'd just lost her best friend. Oh, yeah, that was right—she had.

Cassidy went straight home after the memorial service. She told herself it was to take care of her cats, but she knew Lulu and Bess could get along for days without her. Well, as long as she left out plenty of food and water and had the automatic kitty litterbox plugged in and ready to roll. The truth was she probably needed the cats more than they needed her. It was embarrassing to be nearly thirty-five and single and the owner of two spoiled felines. That wasn't how she'd planned her life to go.

Cassidy called out to the cats as she entered her condo unit. To her relief they both came running. Maybe they sensed her sadness, her need to connect with something living and breathing. She paused to pet the cats, rewarding them both with a kitty treat before she collapsed on the couch and reached for the remote. She knew this was no way to live—and that it did not help with her weight loss goal. But she couldn't help herself.

Abby had always been encouraging Cassidy to get out more. To meet new people and try new things. But Cassidy was good at justifying her choices—she was tired after a rough day at the vet clinic, or she needed to clean house, or she was right in the middle of a really good book. She was full of excuses, but the truth was she had become a real stick-in-the-mud. As Abby had sometimes pointed out, Cassidy had forgotten how to play.

Cassidy's strong work ethic had started early in life. Since she was a teenager, she'd always had summer jobs. It was her way of helping her single mom. But then her mom died shortly after Cassidy started college. With Abby's and Louisa's help and encouragement, Cassidy had managed to put herself through veterinary school. Sure, it had taken nearly ten years with working part-time, but, hey, she'd finished. And shortly after graduation, she'd gotten a job at the best clinic in town. Only half-time, but it would look good on her résumé—if she ever went looking for another job. Dr. Auberon had promised her more hours and she'd been there almost five years, but she was "low vet on the totem pole." Still, her needs were modest and she lived frugally.

Cassidy clicked on the TV, flipping over to the home and garden network—her favorite form of veg-out television. No one would ever guess, judging by her contemporary condo, that she sometimes dreamed of having a real house with a white picket fence and a grassy backyard for pets to run and play. Of course, this dream would be much better with a man by her side. But after having had her heart broken in her early twenties, Cassidy had been very cautious ever since.

She rarely dated, and when she did, she kept her guard up. Abby was the only one Cassidy had confided this to—and that was several years after Conrad had dumped her for a mutual friend, a girl that he'd married within the same year. That had not been easy to swallow back then, and although Cassidy admitted it to no one—not even Abby—it still hurt to think of Conrad sometimes. Not often, but at times when she was feeling tired or weak or sad . . . like now. And as her weight had gone up, her self-esteem had gone down—something else she never spoke of . . . except to Abby.

What was she going to do without Abby? Who would poke and prod her to get a life now? Who would threaten to set up a blind date if Cassidy didn't do something on her own? On Thanksgiving, Abby had good-naturedly dared Cassidy to go out with someone before the end of the year. Cassidy had accepted the dare. But with the end of the year just over a month away and no Abby around to enforce it . . . well, Cassidy felt pretty certain she knew how it would go down. And really, she didn't care.

Louisa hadn't felt up to attending the graveside service following the memorial. She wasn't ready to visit the same cemetery where Adam's remains had been laid to rest less than a year ago. Besides, she told herself as she went into her house, if she really believed what Pastor Gregg had been saying, both Adam and Abby were in heaven now. Not in Pine Grove Cemetery. *Leave the dead to bury their own dead.*

Louisa put on the teakettle, then went to stand in front of the big French doors that led to her perfectly landscaped backyard. Normally she would be filling her bird feeders by now, especially with the chill of winter solidly in the air, but this year she simply hadn't bothered. Hopefully the birds would understand and find someone else's backyard to forage in.

She turned away from the window as the kettle started to whistle. Reaching for a box of chai tea, she paused to smell the spices, but felt no pleasure associated with the familiar aroma. She knew that the loss of everyday pleasures was a symptom of depression. She'd heard it enough times in the grief group that she'd attended for the first month after Adam's death. But she'd also thought she had moved on some. She'd made herself believe that she was coping with it. Then Abby had to go and die.

Louisa felt like she was right back where she'd been last winter, and it didn't help to know that another winter was already knocking on her door. Perhaps it was time to do what her sister Beverly had done—move to Phoenix. Except the idea of baking in the summer and never seeing snow fly in the winter was not that appealing.

As Louisa dipped the tea bag up and down in the hot water, she reminded herself that she had always been a can-do sort of person. Sure, she missed Adam dearly, and she would miss Abby as well. But there had to be more to her life. Good grief, she was only sixty-three! Some people were saying that sixty was the new middle age, not that she bought into that nonsense. Yet for some reason the good Lord still wanted her here . . . although, for the life of her, she could not imagine why.

Who would really care if she were gone? Oh, certainly Matthew and Leah and the grandkids would be saddened at first. But they would get over it in time. And it might even make it easier for them to be living so far away. Nothing over here to tug and pull at them—nothing to feel guilty about.

She closed her eyes and took in a deep breath. "Why *am* I still here?" she whispered. "What is it you want from me?" For a long moment, she stood there in her kitchen with her eyes closed, trying to listen, hoping to hear. But nothing came to her.

She opened her eyes and removed the soggy tea bag from

her tea. Then, as she was dropping it into the trash compactor, she noticed her date book lying open on the counter. Unlike her modern young friends who loved their electronic pads and gadgets, Louisa was old-fashioned. She liked maintaining a date book where she wrote entries and checked regularly. It gave her a sense of stability, as if she had some sort of control of the crazy world she lived in—although she knew that was ludicrous. As she looked at this week, she noticed that Thursday was book group night, and it was supposed to be at Abby's house. Well, of course, that figured. Now that Abby was gone, what would hold the book group together?

By Wednesday, Belinda was able to focus at work, and by midday, she had managed to create a surprisingly nice display in the front window. With Christmas around the corner, she'd decided to use only red, green, or white garments. To accent, she'd added some retro Christmas ornaments—ones she'd gleaned from her grandma's collection many years ago—and some old-fashioned strings of what Emma used to call "gumdrop" lights. She'd also wrapped some boxes with cool retro wrapping paper, and the final effect was delightful.

Normally, she'd be thrilled to see a display coming together so cohesively. Today she simply felt relieved to have the task completed. As she put the remains of the wrapping paper and decorations back into a box, Savannah came over to see. "That looks fabulous," she told Belinda. "Very fun."

Belinda thanked her, then, noticing Clayton Wentworth parking his SUV outside and walking up to her shop, she handed the box to Savannah. "Want to put this away for me?"

"Sure." Savannah glanced toward the door. "Abby's husband?" she whispered.

Belinda nodded as the doorbell jingled, greeting Clayton as he came inside.

"I forgot to give this to you yesterday." He held up a shiny silver bag with a glum expression.

"What's that?"

"Something Abby put together. For book group. I guess you guys were supposed to be meeting at our house this week." He handed her the bag.

"Thanks." Belinda looked into his eyes. "How are you doing?"

He shrugged. "I don't even know."

She sighed. "Yeah, I hear you."

"My brother just retired from the Air Force," he told her. "He wants to stay with me for a while . . . through the holidays."

"That's nice."

"I guess he thinks I need help." He rolled his eyes.

"Well, being alone takes some getting used to." Of course, that was an understatement. After Emma left home for college, Belinda had been a basket case. If Abby hadn't been around, she didn't know what would've become of her.

"Well, Todd's my favorite brother. He'll probably be good company." Clayton was already backing toward the door.

She held up the shiny bag. "Thanks for bringing this."

"I know Abby really wanted you guys to have it." He reached for the door. "I better go."

"Take care, Clayton." Belinda watched as he went back outside. His shoulders were slumped and his head hung down. He looked so lost and sad and alone . . . the same way she felt. Once again she wanted to shake her fist at God, demanding to know why he thought taking Abby away had been such a good idea. Instead she carried the lightweight silver bag to the counter and called Louisa, explaining that Clayton had stopped by and had left a bag for the group.

"What's in it?" Louisa asked.

"I don't know." Belinda peeked in the tissue paper, only to see that the small packages were individually wrapped in more tissue paper. "You know how Abby always loved giving us gifts. She was so crafty. It's probably something she made."

"Book group was supposed to be at her house tomorrow night."

"I know." Belinda sighed. "I was just thinking about that."

"Well, how about if I host the group at my house," Louisa suddenly offered.

"I haven't even finished the book yet," Belinda confessed. "I thought I'd wrap it up this week, but with everything that happened . . . well, I sort of lost interest."

"I didn't finish it either," Louisa said. "To be honest, I found it convoluted and hard to follow, and I really didn't need that."

"No . . ."

"So, can you come?" Louisa's voice grew more hopeful. "I assume this could be our final get-together. Without Abby around to keep us going, well, I'm just not sure what will happen."

"I'd had the same thought." Belinda looked back at the bag. "At least we could find out what's in this bag from Abby and kind of wrap things up—get closure." Belinda cringed at that word—*closure*. What did it really mean?

"So we'll have it at my house," Louisa declared. "I could actually use something to keep me busy right now. I'll even call the others. That is, if you're really okay with this plan."

"Fine by me. Guess I'll see you tomorrow night?"

"Yes. At seven."

As Belinda hung up, she thought this was probably a good idea. Not only did it seem to cheer up Louisa, but it would probably help everyone to sort of say goodbye. Somehow she doubted that anyone would want to continue book group now. Besides missing Abby, four members seemed too small. After fifteen years, perhaps it was time to let it go. She couldn't imagine them continuing without Abby.

As Belinda walked up to Louisa's impressive front door on Thursday night, she could see that Grace and Cassidy were already inside. Louisa had the swankiest home of all the book group members. It wasn't necessarily Belinda's cup of tea since she preferred older homes with more charm and personality, but Louisa's one-story modern home was definitely beautiful—and expensive. Grace had been Louisa's designer, and everything in the house looked coordinated and sleek—like a page from *Architectural Digest*.

"Welcome," Louisa said as Belinda went into the spacious foyer. "You look chic and stylish—as usual."

"Thank you." Belinda attempted a smile as she started to peel off her long coat. "And as usual, everything in here looks beautiful. I sometimes wonder how you manage to keep all these light, neutral colors so clean and crisp, but as always, it all looks perfect, Louisa."

"With no grandkids around . . . and no pets . . . it's not that hard." Louisa took Belinda's full-length leather coat, hanging it in the generous hall closet where even the wooden hangers matched. "Come in and get something to eat. I've been cooking all day. It was good therapy."

Belinda was greeted by the others, and before long they were seated, with filled plates, in Louisa's great room, where the gas fireplace was warmly flickering and several large candles in hurricane glasses were glowing.

"It's so good to see you all," Louisa said. "Thank you for coming tonight. And although I don't know what our future as a book group will be, I must say that I've enjoyed all our years together."

"What do you mean?" Cassidy demanded. "Are we disbanding?"

Louisa shrugged. "I don't know. I guess the group will have to decide."

"Four seems a little small for a book group," Belinda said cautiously. "If someone's gone or forgets, that means just three."

"Maybe we should invite some new people," Grace suggested. "I have a neighbor who's been asking about joining a book group."

"Do you like her?" Cassidy asked.

Grace shrugged. "I don't know her that well. I guess she's okay."

Without much enthusiasm, they discussed the book group and whether or not it should continue. Really, were there many good books they hadn't read? Should they open it to new members and, if so, how many? And should they continue to meet so frequently?

"Reading a book a month sometimes feels overwhelming," Belinda confessed.

"I agree," Grace chimed in.

"Unless you have no life," Cassidy said in a gloomy tone.

Finally, the room grew quiet and Belinda remembered the silver bag. Picking it up, she made a stiff smile. "Clayton brought this by my shop yesterday. I guess Abby had put it together—to give to us tonight."

"What is it?" Cassidy asked.

"I have no idea."

"Well, let's find out," Louisa suggested eagerly.

Belinda reached into the bag, and the first thing she touched felt like an envelope. She pulled it out and read the front aloud. "To My Book Group Friends."

"Please, read it," Grace said anxiously.

So Belinda opened the envelope and extracted a single page. She unfolded it, the room silent. Belinda's hands trembled slightly as she started to read.

Dearest Dear Friends,

I know I don't always tell you all how much I love and appreciate you. Not nearly enough anyway. Life gets busy and I get distracted. But as I finished making these gifts for you tonight, I decided to write down how I feel. And I'm ready for you girls to tell me how corny I am when I read it to you. But that's okay.

You girls have been my closest friends for years. You helped me through my cancer and chemo and radiation. Some of you held my hand when I was afraid, others held my hair while I tossed my cookies. Between the four of you, someone was always there for me. Whether it was bringing us meals, cleaning my house, doing my laundry, even walking my dog—you girls did it. Without you four friends, I don't think I would've made it.

You four women have been my angels over the years. Yes, it's true—in my eyes you, dear friends, are earth angels! I believe God sent you to me because he knew I would need angels—and all four of you came through. And in case I forget to tell you someday, you'll have these little tokens of my love—something to remind you of how grateful I am for my four angel friends. Merry Christmas, Angels!

Love,
Abby

As Belinda slowly refolded the letter, no one spoke, but every-one had tears in their eyes. "Wow . . ." Belinda slid the letter back in the envelope. "I can't believe Abby was calling *us* an-gels—she's the one who was an angel."

"Yeah," Cassidy said quietly. "I was thinking the same thing. And I wish I could be more like her. You know?"

"Me too," Grace said in a shaky voice. "Compared to Abby, I'm not the least bit angelic. Just ask Joel, he'll set you straight."

"I'm no angel." Louisa sadly shook her head, then pointed to the bag. "What else is in there?"

Belinda pulled out a light bundle wrapped in white tissue and tied with gold ribbon. A small gift tag with the name written in gold ink was attached. "To Cassidy," she read as she handed the package to Cass. She removed the others, all wrapped identically with each woman's name on a tag. Finally they were all sitting there with their still-wrapped gifts in their laps.

"Let's see what's inside." Belinda began to untie the ribbon, mindful of how her best friend had so prettily tied it—not so very long ago. The others began to open their parcels as well. The only sound in the room was the rustling of tissue paper being peeled away, followed by some oohs and aahs.

Belinda peered down at the delicate angel ornament in her hand. Made with satin and lace and glitter and ribbons, the small figure was lovely. But it was the hand-painted face on a large wooden bead that captivated Belinda. From the caramel-colored skin to the wavy dark hair and chocolate-brown eyes, this angel was clearly meant to resemble Belinda. She felt the familiar lump growing in her throat as she stared down at the dainty angel. Every detail was perfect.

"Did Abby *know* she was going to die?" Cassidy asked in a tear-choked voice.

Belinda looked up to see the others holding similar—yet

The Christmas Angel Project

different—angels. Each one resembled the woman holding it. Abby had obviously put a lot of time and thought into these gifts. "No, she couldn't have known she was going to die," Belinda told Cassidy. "She had an aneurism. No one can predict something like that."

"But to write that letter—telling us thanks like that," Grace said with surprising intensity. "And to make these angels so that we'd remember her. And calling us her angels . . . doesn't it seem strangely coincidental? Like she had some kind of premonition?"

"It does to me," Louisa declared. "It makes me believe that God's hand was in this."

"That's what I'm thinking." Cassidy held up her angel. "Like this *means* something—like this is something more than a nice memento to hang on my Christmas tree."

"I agree," Grace told her. "It means something more."

"What do you guys think it means?" Belinda asked.

For a long moment, no one spoke, but it was obvious by their expressions that they were all thinking. Thinking hard.

"I think I know what it means," Louisa finally said in a serious tone.

"What?" they all asked together.

Louisa looked from face to face. "I hope I don't sound crazy, but I truly believe I know what this means." She began to describe how depressed she'd been lately—trying to figure out why she was still here. "I was praying to God, asking him why he took Adam and left me here on my own. And why did he take Abby, instead of me? I would've been glad to go join Adam in heaven"—she paused—"instead of having Abby taken, when she had so much life left to live."

Belinda blurted out, "But that doesn't explain why—"

"Let me finish," Louisa said firmly. "I believe that Abby had some kind of premonition—probably from God. She made these angels and wrote that letter to encourage us to—to *become angels*."

"To become angels?" Grace frowned. "What are you saying?"

"I'm saying that Abby was an earth angel," Louisa declared. "She was always touching others—whether with a kind word or a helping hand. You all heard people speaking out at her memorial service this week. Abby's life was nearly twenty years shorter than mine to this point, yet she did far more than I've ever done." She held the angel up by the satin ribbon, watching as the small gray-haired figure slowly spun around. "And I feel personally challenged by *this*. I don't know how many years I have left in this world, but I suddenly feel like I must make better use of my time and energy."

"What do you mean?" Belinda asked.

"I want to be like the angels that Abby described in her letter. And since this is Christmastime, I want to start doing it *now*." Louisa grinned at them. "I want to be a Christmas angel."

"I do too!" Cassidy said eagerly.

"So do I," Grace echoed.

Belinda looked down at the angel in her hand, then slowly nodded. "Okay . . . I want to be a Christmas angel too." As odd as the words sounded to her brain, they resonated deeply with her heart. She did want to be a Christmas angel. "But how do we do it?"

"By creating Christmas miracles," Louisa said. "Angels should be capable of making miracles in other people's lives. Abby did it all the time. That's what we'll do. In honor of Abby's memory."

Suddenly they were all talking, suggesting ways they might help others, good deeds they might do, ways to "pay it forward." By the time they called their meeting to an end, without ever discussing the novel that they all confessed they hadn't finished anyway, their previous sadness and gloom had been edged out by a cautious sort of enthusiasm and energy. Belinda wasn't sure, but as they stood in the foyer, still kicking around some ideas, she felt like Abby might be smiling down on them.

"I think we should meet together regularly," Louisa declared as she helped the women with their coats. "We can report on how our angel work is going and encourage one another."

"Yes!" Cassidy agreed. "Instead of book group, we can have angels' meetings."

"Angels' meetings," Louisa repeated. "I like the sound of that."

They agreed to meet again one week from tonight, with Grace insisting she would host the next angels' meeting in her home. "Maybe it'll inspire me to put up some Christmas decorations," she said a bit glumly. "I haven't felt like it." They all commiserated with her, admitting they hadn't been in the Christmas spirit either.

"I have another idea," Belinda said as she buttoned her coat. "What if we keep this to ourselves—I mean, that we're Christmas angels?"

"You mean we do our angel deeds secretly?" Cassidy asked. "Like a secret Santa?"

"Not exactly," Belinda clarified. "Although that might be fun. I was thinking more about the four of us—the Christmas Angels—maybe we don't tell anyone that part."

"I like that," Grace told her. "Kind of like a secret club."

"Exactly," Belinda told her.

"A club dedicated to Abby's memory," Louisa said.

"Inspired by her," Cassidy added.

As the first meeting of the Christmas Angels broke up and they hurried to their cars in the cold night air, Belinda felt a warm rush of hope going through her. This could be interesting!

5

As Cassidy drove home, she started to concoct her own angel plan. She knew that it would somehow have to involve animals. For as long as Cassidy could remember, she had felt a deep affinity for all creatures. Whether it was goldfish, lizards, or guinea pigs, pets had helped Cassidy through a troubled childhood and unhappy home life. It was why she eventually became a veterinarian. And she knew that helping critters was the same as helping their human owners, because anyone who loved an animal knew how troubling it could be if your pet's health was in peril.

Cassidy suddenly remembered the elderly woman who'd come into the veterinary clinic that morning. Old Mrs. Morgan had paid taxi fare to get her sick cat some much-needed help. She didn't even have an appointment and was barely in the reception area before she tearfully confessed she'd never taken Muffin to a veterinarian before—and that the eleven-year-old cat had no vaccinations whatsoever.

Mrs. Morgan explained it was partly because vet care was

so expensive and partly because, without a car, it was too inconvenient. But she clearly loved Muffin and wanted her kitty to get medical help, even though she became quite distressed when Cassidy insisted the sick feline needed to spend at least one night at the vet clinic in order to get her stabilized. Cassidy had promised to call that evening with updates, which she'd done, and she'd even offered to drop Muffin back at the woman's house when the cat was well enough to return to her home. Hopefully tomorrow.

But now it was all formulating into an angel plan. As Cassidy turned into her condo parking place, she knew exactly what she wanted to do. When she wasn't working, which seemed like most of the time, she would start making "house calls" to elderly people with pets—owners like Mrs. Morgan who couldn't pay for them. Of course, she knew she'd need to clear this with her boss, Dr. Auberon. If he gave his okay, she would figure out a way to make it work. Perhaps he might even want to donate some vaccinations and the basic medications, or at least give her a discount.

As she walked up the stairs to her condo unit, she knew that she needed to respect the group's desire to keep their angel club anonymous. She would explain to Dr. Auberon that this was something she wanted to do during the Christmas season as a gift to disadvantaged pet owners and their pets during the holidays. Hopefully her boss would catch the spirit and want to help.

Cassidy turned on the lights as she went inside, calling out to her own kitties in a sweet tone. Kitties that were thankfully in perfect health, even if they were acting standoffish tonight. Naturally, they wanted to punish her for leaving them alone for the evening. Spoiled felines!

"Fine," she said as she hung up her coat. "Be that way." She removed the soft bundle from her coat pocket, peeling back the tissue paper to examine the beautiful ornament that Abby had made, studying it closely in the bright overhead light. With its pale blue eyes and dishwater-blonde hair (that Abby always called honey-blonde) there was no doubt this angel was meant to resemble Cassidy. Except that it wasn't a chubby angel—that would've been more accurate. This angel was slender and graceful.

Worried that her cats might get ahold of the fragile figure, she hung it on the chain to the overhead fan light. It would be safe there. And every time she passed by, it would remind her of Abby and her angel friends . . . and the project she hoped to get off the ground as soon as possible.

Cassidy kicked off her shoes and sat down on the couch, but as soon as she reached for her iPad, Bess and Lulu came trotting over in a territorial way. Leaping onto the couch and climbing into her lap, they rubbed their furry faces against her hands and the edges of the iPad, making it impossible to read the news story she'd pulled up.

"You cats are so predictable." She closed the iPad cover, pausing to pet her two fickle felines. "If I want you to come to me, you refuse. If I want you to stay away, you won't leave me alone." But then she knew that was the independent nature of a cat. They did as they pleased—the owner could take it or leave it.

She sighed as she leaned her head back into the couch—a man would probably be even harder to live with than cats. Except that a man could visit with her . . . prepare a meal with her . . . rub her tired feet . . . take a walk with her . . . and lots of other things cats were incapable of. Not that there were any fabulous available men around—at least none that she knew of anyway. None that were interested in someone like her. And so it was just her and the cats. The spinster cat lady.

As Grace went into her house, she could hear the TV blaring all the way from the basement. It sounded like a football game. Joel always had ESPN cranked up these days, but even more so when she was out. Without calling down a hello like she knew she should, she quietly closed the door to the basement then went into the kitchen where she pulled out her angel ornament and stared at it.

There was a comfort in knowing Abby had made this for her, but it was no substitute for Abby's friendship. Grace doubted that she'd ever find another friend like Abby. Although she'd been surprised that Belinda had seemed a tad bit warmer tonight, she doubted it was as much an invitation to friendship as it was respect for Abby.

Normally, Grace felt like Belinda didn't much like her. Abby always assured her that was ridiculous. She used to say how it took time to get to know Belinda, and for a while Grace had tried to be friendlier, but it seemed the more she tried, the more distant Belinda became. Finally, Grace decided that Belinda didn't want to be friends. Or else she was a snob. But tonight Belinda had seemed almost sweet. At least for Belinda.

Grace set her angel ornament next to a collection of white candles on the dining table, promising herself that she'd put out some more Christmas decorations over the weekend. And somehow she needed to come up with a strategy to do some kind of angelic work. Grace didn't like to admit this—to anyone, including herself—but she was rather selfish. At least that's what her mother used to tell her. And Joel sometimes hinted at the same thing. The truth was, Grace knew how to keep up a cheerful and generous persona, but her motives were often self-centered. She was great at helping the kind of people who could help her back. Helping someone who couldn't reciprocate—well, that was a new concept to her—something she'd never been comfortable with.

She went to the kitchen for a bottle of sparkling water, noticing that Joel had left a mess. Why was it so hard to put dirty dishes in the dishwasher? As she rinsed them off and shoved them into the appliance, she was not thinking angelic thoughts. Fortunately, Joel wasn't near enough for her to rag on him. Another less-than-angelic behavior. Was she proud of this? Of course not. But, as she'd pointed out to Joel often enough, they both worked outside of the home—wasn't it fair that they both worked *inside* of it too?

As she wiped off the sticky countertops, she knew Joel's standards of housekeeping weren't the same as hers. They never had been. Where it often felt as if he'd been raised by wolves, she probably could pass for an OCD sufferer. But could she help it if she liked a tidy house? A place for everything and everything in its place—what was wrong with that? Why after nearly twenty-five years of marriage did Joel not get this?

Tidy efficiency was especially important in her line of work. A designer's home should be like an example. It should be lovely to look at, a way to gain clients by showing what happens when functionality meets fashion. It simply made sense. But not according to Joel. Her down-to-earth Realtor husband thought a home should look warm and inviting and *lived in*. If that meant shoes on the floor and a newspaper splashed across the coffee table, so much the better. Sometimes it felt like he did those things simply to aggravate her!

Shortly after the twins left for college, the finished basement had become Joel's domain—his man cave. As a result, their paths seldom crossed after the workday. And since they would probably just argue about the twins and their rather uncertain future, maybe that was a good thing. Still, it was lonely. And getting lonelier by the day. Especially with winter around the corner . . . and with Abby gone.

Grace wandered out into their great room. Unlike the chic, stylish space she'd created for Louisa and Adam, this room felt warmer with its earth tones and stone and wood. Joel had insisted upon what he called "casual livability." Naturally, this made sense when the twins were young and at home, but her secret plan had always been to redecorate their empty nest in a stylish contemporary design. Unfortunately, with college tuition and the general economy, finances had been tight. For all Grace knew, she could be stuck with casual livability for a long time.

She sank down into the leather sectional that faced the big stone fireplace, staring into the empty black hole inside of it and wondering if the chimney needed cleaning and how long it had been since they'd lit a fire. She let out a long sigh. When had she become so discontent? And what was she going to do about it? She thought of the angel pact that had been made tonight. It had seemed a good idea at the time, but in the light of day, would she really be able to do anything about it? Anything that mattered or made any difference? And, if so, what would it be?

As she sipped her water, she wondered what Abby would do. Of course, that was ridiculous. Abby would simply keep doing what Abby had been doing all along. Reaching out to everyone around her, loving on everyone, helping everyone, just being Abby—*the earth angel*.

More than anyone Grace had ever known, Abby had been almost completely unselfish. Perhaps that was what had continued to draw Grace to her over the years. If only Grace could be more like her. But it seemed too hard. And now her example was gone. Why bother trying?

Louisa felt a slight spring in her step as she cleaned up after book group, aka their first Christmas Angels' meeting. Getting the girls together tonight had definitely been a step in the right direction. It had been so fulfilling to see their faces light up as they discussed their plan to become earth angels.

As she sealed a plate of leftovers with plastic wrap, some doubts started creeping into her thoughts. What if she'd over-stepped some invisible line? Claiming she knew they were sup-posed to transform themselves into Christmas angels was a bit presumptuous. And yet it had felt so right. Still, as she turned on the dishwasher, she wasn't so sure. What if she wasn't up to the task herself? It was one thing to talk the talk—something altogether different to walk the walk. It would be humiliating to admit to her friends that she had failed at the very idea she'd suggested.

"I will *not* fail," she declared as she rinsed the sink. Yet, as she turned out the kitchen light, more doubts washed over her. What did she have to offer . . . to anyone? She was sixty-three and had never pursued a real career. How could someone like her be of any help to anyone? And yet she had presumed to take the lead with her friends tonight, acting as if she were completely comfortable with what was now feeling like the impossible dream. What had she been thinking?

As she walked through her stylish home, she felt like a phony. Most people assumed she was wealthy, and she seldom bothered to set the record straight. The truth was, she and Adam had lost almost everything in the recent economic slump. Their lovely home was under water, and sometimes—in her most honest moments—she felt that Adam's heart attack had been related to the stress of losing their retirement funds. The only person she'd ever confessed any of this to was Abby. Now her confidante and friend was gone.

As Louisa turned off lights in her house, she prayed, asking God to help her and to teach her how to be an earth angel. After noticing a light still on in the room that used to be her art studio, she went back to turn it off. But when had she turned it on? Before flipping the switch, Louisa glanced around the neglected studio, the neatly arranged shelves of art supplies. A wall of windows. The blank canvases leaning against an old buffet, with various artifacts and items from nature as well as jars of paintbrushes on top.

Everything was ready and waiting for the artist to arrive and go to work. Such a waste. She was about to turn out the light when she noticed a faded old flyer atop a stack of sketch pads. She picked it up, scanning it and trying to remember why she'd kept it. The flyer was about an art therapy program offered by Pine Grove Parks and Recreation.

Now she remembered having a phone conversation with a woman named Fran—not too long before Adam passed away. Louisa had inquired about the program, explaining how she'd had an interest in helping with something like that. She had promised to stop by the park and rec building, and Fran had promised to send out a flyer. Fran had kept her promise, but Louisa had not. Perhaps it wasn't too late.

Belinda had tossed and turned all night, finally waking up on the cusp of an interesting dream. As she dressed for work, she reran the dream through her head. She'd been in some sort of a gymnasium that had a bunch of metal drums, the kind that oil was shipped in. The drums were filled with random items of clothing. Nothing was very nice or interesting, and some of the items, like frying pans and bath mats, weren't clothes at all, but somehow she was supposed to use the contents of those barrels to clothe about a dozen pretty girls for an important fashion show. As soon as she'd get an outfit put together, it would all start falling apart. Very frustrating.

As she walked to town, she wondered what the dream meant. The idea of doing a fashion show was rather appealing. She'd never actually done something like that before, but with the clothes in her shop, it wouldn't be difficult. Certainly much easier than using what was in those fifty-five-gallon barrels. But what would be the point of giving a fashion show? To get business perhaps? Yes, that wasn't a bad idea. But weren't fashion shows usually meant to be fund-raisers? That's when it hit her—a fund-raiser fashion show could be her angel project. But how would it work? What would be a good cause to donate to?

Belinda had several nonprofits she contributed to, but none of them seemed quite right for a fashion show. She wanted something she felt really connected with—something she could care about and really throw her energy into. Isn't that what an angel project should be like?

As she unlocked the front door of Glad Rags, she noticed the city workers finishing up with putting the Christmas decorations on the lampposts. The town was starting to look quite festive. Even her shop, with its colorful display, was looking rather cheery. Belinda wished that she felt as cheery as it looked.

She went inside and started turning on lights, cranking up the heat, and generally straightening what was already a nice, tidy shop. She turned on her music, a handpicked selection of jazz and alternative tunes, then went into her office to do some bookwork and check on the internet for good deals on quality resale garments. This was her early-morning routine. Customers rarely came in this time of the day, and if they did, she'd hear the bell jingling and go out there.

She had just finished up a few things when she decided to check her email. She dumped the usual spam pieces and then opened something from a sender she didn't recognize. It appeared to have been sent several days ago, but she hadn't checked the shop's email account since Abby's death.

Dear Ms. Michaels,

I'm the new principal at McKinley High. One of my faculty members mentioned your name, explaining that you run a thrift shop that's quite popular with young people. I'm sad to admit that many of our female students are both fashion- and financially challenged. I find this very frustrating.

May I be so bold as to ask if you would ever consider partnering with our school in some kind of a fashion project? I honestly don't know how this would play out, but I feel so sad when I see some of these girls trudging around in outfits that could make a streetwalker blush. We do have a dress code here, but I'm discovering it was rarely enforced by the previous principal and, not wanting to become the "Nazi principal," as one girl called me yesterday, I'm hesitant to be overly hard-nosed about this. I know I'm probably asking for a miracle here, but I thought I'd give it a try. Any help is appreciated.

Thanks,
Carey Trellis

Belinda reread the email, and thanks to her weird dream, she immediately began toying with the idea of doing a fashion show at McKinley High. On one hand, it seemed crazy . . . but on the other hand, who knew? Maybe it could be a fund-raiser? Or even a way to help guide the fashion-challenged girls? She wasn't sure. But she was willing.

The more she thought about how much Emma and her friends had liked shopping at Glad Rags, she wondered if there might even be more she could do for these girls. But what exactly? Well, she decided, if nothing else she would continue this conversation with the frustrated principal. And she had to give the woman credit—most principals probably wouldn't go to this effort. Certainly not old Mrs. Crandall (aka Mrs. Cranky back when Belinda's daughter was at McKinley). Belinda had always been supportive of community involvement in the local schools. Just because Emma had moved on was no reason for her to stop.

So she emailed Carey back, saying she would love to help her with her fashion-challenged girls. She even mentioned her fashion show idea and how she'd like to do some kind of fundraiser. By the time she hit Send, she felt slightly enthused. This might actually be fun. Well, unless it turned out to be a giant headache. And that was possible. Belinda knew, from her own daughter and her friends, how fickle adolescents could be about fashion. It could be like walking through a nuclear minefield. Was she really up for the challenge?

6

Cassidy had felt hopeful as she went into the vet clinic on Friday morning, but by the time she finished her four-hour shift, her spirits had sunk considerably. Dr. Auberon seemed determined to play the role of Mr. Scrooge in her idea of offering free pet health care to the needy.

"If I start giving away my services to *some* clients, what will the others say?"

"But I'm the one who'd be doing the work," she'd reminded him.

"What you do in your spare time is your choice, but don't use the name of this vet clinic when you do it."

"So you don't even want to donate any supplies?" she'd asked meekly.

His answer had been to glower at her. As a result, she didn't even bother to ask him about discounting Mrs. Morgan's bill for Muffin. She knew what his answer would be. Instead, she stopped by the reception desk and told Marsha that she wanted to cover that bill herself.

"That's awfully nice of you." Marsha smiled as she ran Cassidy's debit card.

"I'd appreciate it if you didn't mention it to anyone," Cassidy said quietly, "especially Dr. Auberon."

Marsha nodded knowingly. "I understand."

Cassidy took the cardboard cat carrier outside, where the wind was blowing fiercely. Using her coat to cover the case, she hurried to her car. She spoke soothingly to Muffin as she slid the carrier into the backseat, leaving her coat over it as insulation against the cold. Shivering as she drove across town, she continued to talk to Muffin, assuring her that she would soon be reunited with her owner.

It took about fifteen minutes to get to Mrs. Morgan's apartment complex. Although the single-story building looked cheaply built, there was a friendly quality to it, with various pieces of plastic outdoor furniture and flowerpots with fake flowers and outdoor ornaments in front of the units. To Cassidy, it looked like the tenants enjoyed living here. Unlike at her condominium complex, where the units all looked almost exactly the same—stark and tidy to comply with their lease agreements.

With her coat still draped over the cat carrier, she hurried up to apartment 17 and knocked on the door. As she waited, she looked at a collection of garden gnomes gathered around a small bench that looked a bit wobbly.

"There you are," Mrs. Morgan exclaimed as she opened the door wide. "I've been anxiously waiting. Come in, come in." She waved Cassidy into the rather small, crowded front room and pointed to the coffee table. "Go ahead and set that down there. And you covered Muffin with your coat." She smiled at Cassidy. "You are a kind girl."

Cassidy removed her coat then opened the box. "Muffin needs

to take it easy," she said quietly, reaching into her pocket for the prescribed antibiotics. "And she needs to take one of these in her food, three times a day until they're all gone."

"One pill three times a day," Mrs. Morgan repeated.

"Until every single pill is gone," Cassidy stressed. "Otherwise Muffin could get sick again. Even sicker than before."

"I understand." Mrs. Morgan reached for her purse. "How much do I owe you, dear?"

Cassidy made an uncomfortable smile. "It's, uh, it's been taken care of."

"Taken care of?" Mrs. Morgan looked stunned. "What do you mean?"

"Sometimes there are, uh, people who help out at the vet clinic—you know, because they want to. Muffin is such a dear cat that someone wanted to help her."

"Well, bless that kind person's heart." Mrs. Morgan beamed at Cassidy as she closed her purse. "And since you came all this way to bring Muffin home to me, I have made you some soup."

"Soup?"

"Did you already have your lunch?"

"No, actually, I haven't. I just got off work and—"

"Then right this way, missy. I made potato and sausage soup—the same recipe my mother used to make. With real cream too." Mrs. Morgan led Cassidy into the tiny kitchenette where a small chrome-and-plastic dinette—straight out of the fifties—was set with two places, complete with colorful Fiesta dinnerware. "You sit down and I'll ladle out our soup."

"It smells good." Cassidy sat down in a chair and gazed around the interesting kitchen. Everything in here looked collectible. "I love your kitchen," she told Mrs. Morgan. "I mean all your interesting things—the dishes and canisters and pans and everything. It's really cool."

"You sound like my grandson," Mrs. Morgan said as she placed a steaming bowl in front of Cassidy. "He's always saying, 'Don't get rid of any of these old things, Grandma.' He tells me they're valuable." She laughed as she sat down with her own bowl. "This old junk?"

"He's right," Cassidy told her. "I love this style."

"I've had it since I was young and newly married. Probably about your age." She peered curiously at Cassidy. "How old are you, anyway?"

Cassidy told her, and Mrs. Morgan blinked in surprise. "Well, I never would've guessed. You look much younger."

After Cassidy thanked her, Mrs. Morgan bowed her head and said a sweet, short blessing, adding on a special thank-you to Muffin's benefactor before they began to eat.

"This is delicious," Cassidy told her after the first bite.

"I'm so glad you like it." Mrs. Morgan handed her the bread basket. "I didn't bake these biscuits myself, but my neighbor did. Only this morning. We're always exchanging food in these apartments. Sort of like one big happy family. Well, mostly, anyway. There are a few cranky grouches that live here. We try to stay out of their way."

"Do many people in this apartment house have pets?" Cassidy asked.

"Oh, my, yes. Helen Downs has three cats. Gordon Moore has a little boxer mix named Buster. Gladys Fortner has a parrot." She continued to list the tenants with pets, often mentioning the animals by name.

"Do any of your friends have trouble getting their pets to the veterinarian?"

Mrs. Morgan frowned. "We all live on fixed budgets here. Social Security and such. Feeding a pet is an additional expense. Paying for vet bills . . . well, it can be difficult."

Cassidy explained her idea, and Mrs. Morgan's eyes lit up. "That would be so wonderful. What a lovely thing to do. The Auberon Animal Hospital is to be commended. Such kind people."

Cassidy wasn't sure how to respond, but remembering Dr. Auberon's comments about keeping her volunteer work separate from the clinic, she knew she had to explain. "Actually, this is not part of Auberon Animal Hospital. This would be a mobile veterinarian that's financed by private donations." Okay, that wasn't a lie. Cassidy would be privately funding this out of her own pocket, and it would certainly be mobile, since she'd be working out of her car.

"Well, I think it's wonderful! I can't wait to tell my neighbors about it. I know that Gordon has been worried about Buster lately. Seems he's got some sort of skin problem."

"Maybe I could take a look at him after lunch," Cassidy offered.

They continued visiting as they ate, and by the time they had finished, Cassidy felt like they were old friends. "Thank you for the soup, Mrs. Morgan," Cassidy said as she was getting ready to leave.

"Please, call me Dorothy," she said as she walked Cassidy to the door, pointing outside and to her right. "Gordon's apartment is right down there—number 22. Just knock on his door and tell him I sent you to see about Buster."

"Thanks." Cassidy zipped up her parka.

"Thank you!" Dorothy said happily. "And, please, feel free to stop in anytime. Anytime at all. We can have lunch together again."

Cassidy smiled. "I might have to take you up on that."

"I hope you will," she said eagerly. "Now don't disappoint me."

Cassidy waved goodbye before going down to apartment 22, where some whirligigs were stuck into a flowerpot with a dead plant. She knocked on the door, and when a short, bald man answered, she quickly explained.

"Dorothy sent you here to see Buster?" He scratched his chin with a doubtful expression.

"I'm a volunteer veterinarian, and I do house calls," she said. "Dorothy thought Buster needed a checkup for his skin problem. Would you like me to take a look?"

He still looked uncertain, and she suggested he give Dorothy a call, but he said he had no phone because he couldn't afford it. So she further explained about Muffin being sick and going to the vet clinic, and how she'd brought Muffin home.

"Well, then, why didn't you say so?" He grinned as he opened the door wider. "Dorothy told me about the kind vet lady who was going to deliver Muffin back home. That must be you."

His apartment, unlike Dorothy's, was rather barren and smelled pretty doggy. But since she was accustomed to pet smells, Cassidy ignored it as she removed her parka and hung it on a hook by the door. Before long she was examining Buster. "It looks like eczema," she told him. "Perhaps aggravated by a food allergy. May I see what dog food he's been eating?"

Gordon showed her a large bag of cheap dog food and, after reading the ingredients, Cassidy suspected it was the corn that might be bothering the old dog. She explained this and suggested Gordon try a rice and lamb blend instead. She guessed by Gordon's expression that this might be a problem.

"I plan to come back over here tomorrow," she told Gordon. "I'll bring you a sample of the food I'm recommending, as well as some ointment for Buster."

Gordon's face lit up. "That'd be helpful to try a sample. Then I can see if it really is the food. Buster's been eating this same food for years. Can't understand why it would be a problem now."

She explained how allergies sometimes occurred after resistance to allergens wore down over the years, and Gordon nodded with understanding. "I guess I have heard about that before with humans. Didn't know it was true with dogs as well."

"So I'll stop by here tomorrow afternoon," she told him. "And you can let your neighbors with pets know that I'll be available."

"There's another sick dog," Gordon said quickly. "Hank Johnson's German shepherd, Bobby, is off his feed. Hank seems real worried about the dog. You think you could go have a look?" He told her the apartment number and she hurried on down to check on Bobby.

One thing led to another, and by the time Cassidy left the apartment building, she'd seen five pets. She made notes for what they needed and promised to return tomorrow afternoon with the various meds and supplies.

As she drove home, she was a little concerned about how she'd manage to pay for the necessary items, but she decided that angels probably didn't worry about such things—they probably just trusted that the Lord would provide. Anyway, she was determined to do what she could to help the five pets and their owners to live more comfortably. After that, well, she'd have to see.

7

On Saturday morning, Louisa went to meet with Fran Jacobs, the manager of the parks and recreation programs. It didn't take long to figure out that they needed help.

"Our budget got so cut back last year, the art therapy class never had a chance to get off the ground," Fran said in a dismal tone. "We can't afford to hire anyone, let alone provide art supplies. It's a challenge just keeping the lights on here, and I've had to let several employees go. Many of our kids' programs have been cut. And next year's budget looks even worse."

"I wanted to volunteer," Louisa explained. "And I can provide art supplies. At least to start with."

"Really?" Fran looked relieved. "You'd do that?"

"All I need is the space to do it. Although I suppose I could do it from my home."

"We do have space," Fran assured her. "That's no problem. And there might still be a few art supplies in the arts and crafts room."

"Do you think there are people who'd want to participate in art therapy?" Louisa asked tentatively.

"We had a lot of calls last winter. I even saved their numbers in the hope that we'd get something pulled together."

"Well, I don't have actual experience in teaching art therapy, but I did take a couple of classes in college—long ago—and I was always interested in it." She made a sad smile. "I suppose I've been in need of it myself this past year."

Before long, Louisa had a list of phone numbers and was taking a tour of the building, including the arts and crafts room, which she'd reserved for Thursday mornings.

"I wonder if next week is too soon to start," Louisa mused as they walked back to the main office. "So many people get blue during the holidays . . . Maybe it would be good to offer them an outlet before Christmas."

"Feel free to start the class whenever you like," Fran told her. "But I won't get it onto the website or the schedule until after the New Year."

"Well, I'll give these folks a call and see what the interest level is," Louisa said as she was getting ready to leave. "Perhaps they've all moved forward in their lives by now."

However, when Louisa got home and started to call the numbers, informing the people about her class that was starting on Thursday morning, she was surprised to discover that several of them were eager to come. She explained that although she was an artist and knew a bit about art therapy, it would be new to her as well. "But hopefully we can all learn and heal together," she assured them.

By the time she finished she had seven people who had committed to come. Seven! She could hardly believe it. As she went to work packing up the various paints and brushes and sketch pads and canvases, she felt hopeful. Perhaps she would have a useful role in this life after all. That is, unless she failed at this. She knew that was entirely possible. What did she really know about art therapy? She'd spent the past year avoiding her painting studio and wallowing in her sorrows—what made her think she could help anyone now? Wouldn't it be like the blind leading the blind?

❖⟫⟫⟫••❖••⟪⟪⟪❖

As Grace sat in her design studio on Monday morning, staring at a set of blueprints that didn't really make sense, she felt stuck. Not stuck as far as the design she was supposed to be working on—although she did feel uninspired. And not stuck as far as her marriage and mixed-up children went—although she certainly had no idea of what to do about either of those situations. Mostly she felt stuck in her commitment to partner with her book group friends, masquerading as an "angel" when she knew better.

Really, what had she been thinking? She picked up her phone, deciding to call Louisa and beg out of this preposterous agreement. She would say she was too busy and with the holidays had too much on her plate. Surely her friends would understand. She was about to hit speed dial for Louisa when she noticed the angel ornament that she'd brought to work with her today— hoping it would inspire her to greatness.

There it was, lying facedown on a pile of old junk mail. Not very inspiring. She picked up the angel and studied its sweet face, wishing that she would hear Abby's voice coming down from on high, telling her what to do. Of course, Abby would probably say something like: "Only God can tell you what to do, Grace. He wants to direct your path—if you'll just take the time to listen."

Grace closed her eyes for a few seconds, imagining that she was taking the time to listen, but knowing in her heart that she wasn't. She had never been the type to slow down and contemplate or meditate or whatever it was that helped people to hear God speaking to them. Did God actually speak to people, or did they simply imagine it? She wasn't sure. Wasn't sure she even wanted to find out. Because if God did speak to her, he would probably voice his severe disappointment—the same way her parents used to do. Nothing she did was ever good enough then. Why would it be good enough now?

She opened her eyes and started to lay the angel back down on the stack of ignored mail when she noticed a familiar envelope sticking out of the pile. It wasn't really junk mail; it was from the Habitat for Humanity folks—probably a solicitation for a year-end donation, since Grace had already told them she was useless with hammers and saws. For some reason she was curious about the ivory envelope's contents.

She opened it and was surprised to see that it wasn't a form letter like she'd expected. Instead it was an invitation to participate in a special holiday project. Local interior designers were being asked to help decorate the three newest Habitat homes in time for a Christmas open house. Perhaps this was the angel project she'd been looking for! She glanced at the date and was dismayed to see that the letter was several weeks old. Would it be too late to participate?

Without wasting another minute, she decided to call the number at the bottom of the letter. Being featured in a holiday open house—even for Habitat—would be good PR. When she finally connected with the woman in charge, she was pleased to hear that they still needed a decorator. "It's for the living rooms for all three homes," Julia Abernathy informed her. "We thought that Wallace and Stein Interiors had taken them on, but they were forced to bow out late last week and I've yet to find another designer."

"Oh, I'd love to do those rooms," Grace said eagerly. Never mind that she still didn't have her own Christmas decorations up—she wanted to do this.

"Then we'd love to have you do it. The open house is scheduled for the Sunday before Christmas—that's barely two weeks from now. Can you pull it together by then? Remember, it's for *three* living rooms."

"I'm sure they're not large rooms."

"No, not at all. The homes are all between 1,000 and 1,200 square feet."

"That's no problem." Grace imagined setting up faux trees and hanging garlands and placing various decorations here and there—and setting her placard out for everyone passing through to see. Piece of cake!

"That's fabulous! Such a relief. After Wallace and Stein informed me they couldn't afford it, I was afraid the living rooms would look so barren compared to the rest of the houses' interiors. The other designers have already been hard at work."

"Well, I'll get right on it too," Grace said positively. "As soon as today, even." She wondered why a large firm like Wallace and Stein couldn't afford a few Christmas decorations. But their loss would be her gain and her chance to shine, since she had all sorts of decorations, both at home and in the stockroom. Easy-peasy. "So should I assume the Christmas decorations will be on loan in the houses?"

"Well, that's up to you, but I must say that donating Christmas decorations would be a nice little perk for the families. Although I'd understand if you were putting something special in the rooms—you know, for the open house. Of course, all the furnishings will be donated. That's what makes this whole thing so special. Imagine these families getting a fully furnished home right before Christmas. It's the first time we've been able to do something this big. And I can't tell you how exciting it's been."

"Furnishings?" Grace felt a wave of concern.

"Yes. Didn't you read the letter? The furnishings are being donated as a Christmas blessing to the three Habitat families."

Grace's mouth went dry. "Oh."

"Didn't you understand?"

"Yeah, sure. Of course," Grace said quickly. "I was so focused on the Christmas decorations . . . I hadn't given the actual furnishings and designs much thought yet."

"Well, as I said, none of the rooms are very big. And most of the designers are seeking donations from various businesses in town, although a few have donated from their own warehouses. And, of course, you're allowed to shop for free in our Habitat Restore. That's always fun—seeing an old piece put to use."

"Right . . ." Grace wanted to backpedal now, to admit she'd made a stupid mistake, but her pride kept her from speaking up.

"So you're okay with it?" Julia asked hopefully. "It would mean so much to have all three homes completely finished in time for the open house. We plan to have refreshments and a Santa and music and all sorts of festivities that day."

"Yes," Grace said mechanically. "I'm okay with it." But as soon as she hung up, she felt sick. Had she actually agreed to furnish three living rooms—and decorate them for Christmas—all out of her own pocket? What had she gotten herself into? And what would Joel have to say about it?

By Tuesday, Belinda and the principal at McKinley High had exchanged several emails and come up with a pretty good plan. Belinda was impressed at how much Carey seemed to care for her students. She really had their best interests at heart. In fact, it was her idea to put together a holiday fashion show that would utilize the teenage girls as models. The fund-raising proceeds, they'd both decided, could go into the high school's academic scholarship fund—the same fund that had helped Emma to get into a more expensive college when she'd graduated from McKinley a few years ago.

Carey invited Belinda to come in after school on Tuesday afternoon to go over the details and to meet the girls that Carey was recommending as models. Carey had warned Belinda that the girls would not be stereotypical fashion models, but would come in various shapes and sizes. And Belinda had responded by saying she thought that was a great idea and that her shop could accommodate them.

As prearranged, Belinda went to the administration's conference room at 3:30. She could hear the young voices as she approached the room. Hopefully the girls would be excited about the prospect of modeling. Although you never could tell with adolescents. The last thing she wanted was to have to twist arms to get cooperation. In fact, she'd decided if she couldn't get them on board today, she would put on the brakes and look for a different sort of project.

As she entered the conference room, she observed there were about a dozen teen girls, but she didn't see anyone who looked like the principal among them. Where was Carey?

"Hello, ladies," a deep voice said. The girls grew quiet, looking toward the door as an attractive African American man strolled into the room. Belinda wondered if he was a teacher— not one who was here when Emma was in school, because Belinda knew she would've remembered him. Was he in the wrong room?

Instead of excusing himself and leaving, he went to the head of the table. Dressed in a handsome charcoal gray suit with a burgundy tie, he smiled at everyone. "I'm so glad you could all make it." He looked over to where Belinda was standing and his smile grew even brighter. "And you must be Ms. Michaels." He went over to shake her hand. "I'm Mr. Trellis, McKinley High's new principal."

"You're a man?"

The room broke into giggles along with a couple of snarky remarks.

He grinned. "Hey, thanks for noticing."

"But your name," she stammered. "I assumed you were a woman."

He laughed. "Sorry about that. I didn't even think. Please tell me you're not going to walk out on this idea because I'm a man. I happen to have great respect for fashion." He looked over at the students. "Don't I, girls?"

This set them off to giggling even more. It was obvious that the girls were as enamored of him as she was feeling. More comments were exchanged, and one girl mentioned that Mr. Trellis was so into appearances that they sometimes called him the Fashion Nazi. Of course, based on some of these girls' outfits, Belinda couldn't blame him. She never would've let Emma out the door looking like some of them.

"See what I mean?" he jokingly told Belinda. "This is a tough crowd." He took a moment to introduce Belinda, explaining their collaboration to hold a fashion show that would help with the scholarship fund. "Who knows, maybe some of you will be the recipients of a scholarship." Then he excused himself to go attend to some other business, and Belinda was all by herself with the roomful of girls.

Trying to conceal her embarrassment over her wrong as-sumption about Carey, she nervously launched into her plans for the fashion show. But as she talked, she could tell that some of the girls were not showing much, if any, enthusiasm. In fact, the longer she went on about it, the more she knew she was losing them. They probably wished that it was Carey leading this meeting—not her. For that matter, Belinda did too.

Belinda paused for a moment, looking out over the girls' bored faces as they slumped like sloppy bags of grain in the conference chairs. They clearly did not want to be here. And they probably had no interest in modeling clothes from her shop. No matter that every single one of them could use a serious makeover!

It suddenly became very important that she not lose them— not a single one. Not only for Carey's sake, although to be honest she really wanted to impress that fine-looking man. But seeing these girls and the way they were dressed—in shabby, ill-fitting clothes—made her truly want to help them. The same way she used to help Emma and her friends when she'd first started up Glad Rags. And she wanted to do it in such a way that they wouldn't even know they were being helped.

"So this is the plan," she said loudly, to be heard over some of the chattering that was developing between the girls. "Anyone who volunteers to model for this fashion show will get to *keep* one of the outfits she wears."

"We get to keep the clothes?" one of the girls said with interest.

"That's right. You'll need to wear several outfits, but you can choose the one you like best to keep as a thank-you for cooperating."

"Cool," a girl with frizzy red hair said.

"Glad Rags has some pretty rad stuff." A skinny blonde with a tattoo of a thorny rose on her wrist made a shy smile.

Suddenly the girls started chattering among themselves— and with her too. It sounded like they were totally down with the whole thing. She handed them forms to fill out regarding their sizes, even providing them with a couple of dressmaker measuring tapes to fill in some of the lines. For about an hour, they all worked together, measuring and filling out the forms. Although some of the girls were giving others a bad time over some measurements, Belinda reminded them that there was no "perfect" size and that everyone would be a great asset to the fashion show. "Beauty comes in all shapes and sizes," she declared.

"Yeah, that's easy for you to say," a girl named Remmie told her. "You're gorgeous."

"Yeah," another said. "You were probably a professional model."

"As a matter of fact, I was a skinny, awkward teen," she told them. "Girls made fun of my height and my braces, and I never even went out on a date until after high school."

This really seemed to win them over, and by the time they finished with the forms, it felt like they were all becoming friends. At the end of the meeting, she explained that she'd secured the Amber Room for the fashion show, and that it was scheduled for the Saturday before Christmas. She held up the tickets that Savannah had printed for her this morning, even taking the time to hand-number each one and bundle them into twenty packets of ten.

"I'm going to give a prize to the girl who sells the most tickets," she told them. "A hundred-dollar gift certificate for my shop."

Suddenly the girls were clamoring for ticket bundles. Wanting to keep track of who sold what, Belinda got Remmie to write down the numbers on the bundles as she handed them out to the girls. When it was all done, she explained how they should report to her every few days how many they'd sold. "We have limited capacity, so you don't want to procrastinate. And I'll let you know when the room is full up." She gave them a positive smile. Hopefully the Amber Room would be sold out, but she didn't really expect it.

She felt like she'd covered everything, but decided to invite the girls to ask questions. One asked what they would do for hair and makeup, and she told them that she'd have some volunteers on hand to help. A few more practical questions were asked, and then a heavyset girl who'd been pretty quiet spoke up. "Why are you doing this?" she demanded. "Is it cuz you feel sorry for us?"

Belinda just smiled at her. "The truth is, I needed something to distract me from feeling sorry for myself." She briefly explained about the death of her best friend, Abby. Not surprisingly, many of them knew who Abby was, and several had been in her kindergarten class. "Besides that, my daughter Emma went to school here. She graduated three years ago, and I used to have such fun helping her and her friends put outfits together. I guess I missed that." Several of the girls remembered Emma, and by the time Belinda was leaving the conference room, she felt like she'd made a whole roomful of young friends.

"So how did it go?" Carey Trellis asked, falling into step with her as she walked through the courtyard.

She smiled at him. "I think it went really well."

He looked relieved. "That's great to hear."

"I mean, after I got over the shock of you not being a woman," she teased.

He laughed. "Sorry about that. I wondered if you thought that while we were emailing back and forth. You seemed so open and friendly, like you were chatting with a girlfriend."

She frowned to remember how she'd imagined that she and

Carey were going to become friends. "That might've been because I was missing my best girlfriend." She quickly explained about Abby.

"I'm sorry." His dark brown eyes looked truly sympathetic. "That's hard."

"But the girls in there were great." She nodded. "I think they're all on board."

His eyes lit up. "Impressive. To be honest, I wasn't so sure they'd agree so easily. You must have the magic touch."

She decided not to mention her little incentives. Better to let him think she was simply amazing. "Well, thanks for inviting me to help with this," she said. "I think it'll be fun." She forced her eyes away from his face—worried that he might figure out that she was ogling him. But as she looked down, she couldn't help but notice that his wedding ring finger was conspicuously bare. Not that it meant anything. Lots of men didn't like to wear rings.

"So, I think I heard that you're single," he said as he paused on the edge of the courtyard, looking out toward the parking lot.

She glanced back at him, feeling embarrassed for the second time. He'd obviously caught her staring at his ring finger. "Well, yes," she said crisply. "I have been single for quite some time. It's no secret."

He nodded with a somber expression. "I lost my wife to cancer several years ago."

"I'm sorry." She could see the sadness in his eyes.

"That's one of the reasons I decided to relocate to a new town and new job—I thought a change of venue might help me move on."

"Has it helped?"

He shrugged. "I think so . . . but it's still not easy."

Her heart went out to him. "I know. It wasn't easy when my

husband left me. Although he didn't die—he just found a new wife." The truth was, she thought it would've been easier if Byron *had* died, but she had no intention of saying that.

"I'm sorry . . . that must've been hard."

"Thank you, Mr. Trellis."

"Please, call me Carey." He smiled. "At least when the kids aren't around."

"Only if you call me Belinda."

He stuck out his hand and they shook. "Thanks for what you're doing for these girls, Belinda. Hopefully it will make a difference in the way they see themselves."

She nodded eagerly. "I think it will. I'm actually really excited about this."

They promised to remain in touch by email, and she even handed him a small bundle of tickets to sell. "Let me know if you need more," she called out as she headed across the parking lot. As she walked, she felt a lightness in her feet—something she hadn't experienced in years.

8

After only three days, Grace knew she was in way over her head with the Habitat project. Getting the local furniture stores to consider donating three rooms of furniture right before Christmas was like pulling teeth. And the selection of fashionable furnishings at the Habitat Restore was, at best, limited. Despite the fact that she and Camille had been calling all over town, scouring back rooms and warehouses, she had very little to show for it by Wednesday.

"You need to lower your standards," Camille was telling her during their lunch break. "These Habitat houses aren't paying clients. They should be glad to have anything. Even if you get it at Goodwill."

Grace frowned. "But it's a reflection on me as a designer," she pointed out.

"Yeah, but you're doing it for free," Camille reminded her. "What's the big deal?"

"The big deal is that my name is on it and I want it to be nice." Grace crumbled up her brown bag as she stood. "Keep calling around. You've got the list I gave you." She tossed her bag into the trash and sighed. "I'm going out to do some more schmoozing. Maybe I'll get lucky." Although as she pulled on her coat and scarf, she doubted it.

Reaching for her bag containing the floor plans and room sketches she'd put together for the Habitat rooms on Monday, she wondered why she'd even bothered with them. It wasn't as if she was going to find the individual items that she felt would make the rooms really sparkle and shine. She would be lucky if she rounded up three decent couches and a few chairs. Why on earth had she ever agreed to this? Oh, yeah, she thought she was only putting up Christmas decorations. That's what she got for moving too fast. Joel had warned her of this very thing plenty of times.

She got into her car, pushing away thoughts of Joel. Naturally, he had thought she was crazy for taking on this impossible task. He'd liked the idea that she wanted to help with Habitat, but he predicted her failure. And that had simply made her more determined to succeed. Somehow she had to pull this off. But it would take a miracle.

Her plan for the afternoon was to hit the less-traditional stores. Even if that meant doing one of the homes only in import items, it could be worth it. She made numerous stops, sharing her story and practically begging for donations, but other than a few odd pieces that she wasn't even sure she could use, she was not making much progress. By the end of the day, she was discouraged and weary. Why had she taken this on?

Not wanting to carry the items she'd foraged around in her car, she decided to drop them off at the nearest Habitat house. Julie Abernathy had given Grace keys to all three homes, and since one of them was on her way home, she decided to stop there. When she noticed an old blue pickup in the driveway, she assumed it was a volunteer worker staying late. But when she went inside, she was surprised to meet the family who would soon become the owners of this house.

"I'm Ginny," the young woman told Grace. "And these are my girls. Hannah is almost three and Holly is six."

"Pleased to meet you." Grace introduced herself, explaining she was the designer in charge of the living room.

"It's so exciting," Ginny said happily. "Not to just get a house but furniture too. I felt like I won the lottery when they told me that."

"Is that for us?" Holly asked with wide eyes as she stared at the glass lamp in Grace's hands. "It's really, really pretty!"

"I—uh—I'm not sure. It might be." She smiled at the little girl. "I'm still working out the plan."

"We never really had much furniture before," Ginny told her. "An old futon that doubled as our couch and my bed. Boxes for end tables. Pillows to sit on."

"We pretended we were gypsies," Holly told Grace.

"That's because we kept having to move," Ginny explained. "One rental house got sold. Then the apartment complex got condemned. Right now we're staying in a travel trailer that's parked at my sister's house. It's been a real challenge." She smiled as she looked around the room. "I still can't believe this is going to be ours."

"We helped to build it," Holly said proudly. "And Mommy has worked on a whole bunch of other people's houses. She knows how to hammer and saw and everything."

"That's how it works," Ginny told Grace as she picked up the smaller girl, who was starting to whine. "You have to live in the same town and keep a job and work on other Habitat houses before they even put you on the list. I got us on the list before, uh . . . ," she lowered her voice as Holly did a somersault across the carpeted room, "before my husband left us. That was right before Hannah was born. But because I had a full-time job and I kept helping on the other Habitat houses, they let me stay on the list." She stroked Hannah's hair, pushing it out of what looked like sleepy eyes. "It's not easy with childcare and stuff. But my sister has helped a lot. She watches the girls for me sometimes."

"We're gonna move in before Christmas," Holly said as she came back to stand with them. "We'll have our own tree and everything."

"Yeah." Ginny nodded eagerly. "We had a rough Christmas last year."

"That's cuz we were moving. We had to stay in Aunt Lisa's attic." Holly made a face. "There were rats up there."

"Not rats," Ginny corrected. "Mice."

"But you could hear them chewing at night," Holly said dramatically. "And they chewed up my kitty."

"The mice chewed a cat?" Grace felt slightly horrified.

"A plush cat." Ginny frowned. "But that was before my dad parked the old travel trailer there for us to stay in. We've been in it this past year."

"It's got mice too," Holly informed Grace.

"We set traps," Ginny told Holly. "The mice are all gone now."

"But it can get awful cold." Holly pretended to shiver.

"Well, I'm sure you're going to love your new home." Grace forced a polite smile. "And I'll do all I can to make it comfortable for you."

"Mommy's favorite color is green," Holly told Grace. "But I like purple. Hannah likes pink."

Grace nodded. "I'll keep that in mind."

"We'll be thankful for anything," Ginny said quickly. "Any

color that you think is good will be much better than what we've had before." She shifted Hannah to the other side. "She's worn out. I should probably get going. It's just that a worker was still here as I was going home, and I asked if I could take a peek." She chuckled. "We're not supposed to look at it once the designers start their work."

"I saw the bed in my room," Holly chirped. "It's beautiful!"

"But we won't peek anymore," Ginny promised.

"I'll lock up when I leave," Grace said as Ginny tugged Holly toward the front door.

"Thank you for all you're doing," Ginny said. "We really, really appreciate it. I can't even say how grateful we are."

"Yeah, thank you!" Holly shouted as they went out.

Grace got the other items from her car, setting them in a corner of the living room and then looking all around. Although the space was relatively small compared to living rooms she usually did, it looked awfully empty right now. Suddenly, she wanted to do whatever it took to fill it with wonderful, beautiful things. Not because of her reputation now, but because she wanted to give Ginny, Holly, and Hannah a delightful place to live. Somehow she had to get it together for them.

Although she'd dressed carefully and meticulously rehearsed her introductory speech, Louisa wasn't prepared for her first art therapy class on Thursday. Nothing could've prepared her for all the emotion that surfaced shortly after she finished explaining the basic concept behind art therapy. Despite trying to appear self-assured and ready to lead these troubled people away from their problems, she was like a fish out of water.

Instead of getting into the drawing project like she'd hoped they would, the small group of people sitting at the big round table only wanted to rehash the grief that they couldn't seem to get past. Finally, at what should've been halfway through their class time, Louisa knew she had to speak up and change the direction. Either that or go home and have a pity party of one—and she didn't intend to do that! But before she opened her mouth, she said a silent prayer. Actually it was more like a desperate cry for help.

"I realize that you're all working through some fairly serious losses," she began carefully, "but I want to remind you that you came here today in search of healing. We want to start moving on. And, as an artist, I believe that art can be very therapeutic to the hurting heart."

Even as she said this, she seriously doubted her own words. She hadn't been able to pick up a charcoal or a paintbrush since Adam passed away nearly a year ago. And when Abby died, Louisa had been determined to give away all her art supplies and call it a day. Yet, here she was—standing before seven total strangers stuck in the midst of their own grief who were looking at her with doubt and mistrust—acting like she had all the answers. It was perfectly ludicrous, not to mention humiliating.

"That might be easier said than done," a young woman said.

"I'm aware of that," Louisa muttered, wishing she'd never volunteered for this impossible class.

"Have you ever taught art therapy before?" a middle-aged woman named Cindy asked skeptically. "Do you even *know* what you're doing?"

"Well, to be honest, this is a new experience for me too."

"Just like the teacher who started this class last year," Cindy said a bit sharply. "She didn't know what she was doing either. That's why the whole thing fell apart. I don't know why I bothered to come. Except that I like the idea of becoming an artist."

"I used to paint color-by-number," an elderly man named Bruce said quietly. "I thought maybe I'd take that up to help me get over losing Ruth this past summer. But I suppose I could do that by myself at home."

"Give Louisa a chance," an elderly woman said sharply. "Maybe she knows more than she's letting on."

Suddenly Louisa's confidence plummeted even lower. She was painfully aware that not only did she know very little about art therapy, she'd never really worked outside of the home before either. Her last real job was waiting tables to help pay for her college tuition, and she'd been lousy at that too. What did she think she was doing?

"I'm sorry," she told everyone, holding back tears of frustration. "You're probably right. I don't really know what I'm doing. I apologize for wasting your time." She started to gather her things, ready to bolt for the door, to run from the building and never come back again.

"Wait," the elderly woman said. "You can't give up like that. You must've come here for a reason. Something made you think you could lead this group. Tell us about yourself, Louisa. Tell us why you're here."

Louisa blinked, setting her large canvas bag down on the table with a clunk. "Well, I—uh—I'm an artist. That's about all I've been in my life. And I used to enjoy painting and drawing and creating—almost on a daily basis. But then my husband, Adam, passed away . . . last January . . . after that, well, I found it difficult—"

"You lost your husband too?" Cindy looked surprised. "Why didn't you just say so?"

"Oh . . ." Louisa frowned. "Yes, I suppose I should've mentioned that earlier. One of my dearest friends also passed away recently. Right after Thanksgiving. I'm still working through that as well."

"And you think painting really helps?" Bruce asked hopefully.

"The truth is, I've been unable to paint or draw or anything. I'd hoped that doing this class would be as therapeutic to me as it would be to all of you."

The room got very quiet now and Louisa wondered if they were as ready to give up on her as she was to give up on herself.

"But you really are an artist?" Cindy asked.

"Yes," Louisa said eagerly. "I brought some of my paintings." She pointed to the stack on the nearby counter. "They're over there."

Suddenly everyone was on their feet, and Louisa began showing them the samples of her work. To her relief, they seemed to like the pieces she'd brought, seemed to appreciate that she actually did know a thing or two about art. Finally, she began to confess to them how much she missed the process of painting.

"Something happens when I paint," she told them. "It's as if part of me disconnects from the world, and my focus goes into whatever I'm working on. If I was troubled by something when I started to paint, I usually forget all about it for a while. And I might even have some fresh ideas for resolving it by the time I finish. Sometimes it feels almost miraculous."

She led them back to the table, knowing that their time was limited now. Just the same, she went around and gave them each a piece of drawing paper and a pencil.

"This is what I want us to do." She removed an old pale blue pitcher from her canvas bag. It had been her mother's and was decorated with roses and leaves. She set it in the center of the table with a clunk. "Draw that."

"It's cracked," Cindy pointed out.

"I know." Louisa sighed to remember the day she'd dropped

the pitcher, then glued it back together. "It's broken. The same way we're all broken. But go ahead and draw it as it is. And don't worry about what your drawing looks like, or how good your drawing skills are. Just do the best you can. It doesn't matter if your picture looks nothing like this pitcher. The important thing is to simply connect with what you're doing. Think about the lines you're putting down. Pretend that it's only you and the pencil and the paper—let yourself go and don't stop drawing until I tell you to stop. And I'll warn you, we don't have much time left in here today."

Some of them went straight to work. Others sat there staring at the pitcher and then down at their blank pages. Louisa quietly worked her way around the table, offering encouragement and some very gentle suggestions—mostly to get them to put the pencil to the paper. Then after about thirty minutes, she called, "Time," and asked them to lay down their pencils.

"Now let's go around the room and share what went through our minds as we drew," she announced. "And, please, don't feel you need to come up with any correct answers. There is no such thing in this group. Simply explain how you felt in the midst of your drawing."

The first one to share was a young man named Rod. Louisa knew that he'd lost his older brother in a motorcycle accident, but he'd been fairly quiet until now. He held up his sketch, which was actually quite good, but mostly he spoke of feeling intimidated about drawing, worried that someone might make fun of him, pointing out that his parents had pressured him into coming today. "I really don't see how this can make anyone feel better."

"Were you able to disconnect with your worries as you drew?" Louisa asked.

"I guess so."

"Then perhaps it wasn't a complete waste." She smiled at him. "And I can see that you have real artistic talent."

His face lit up slightly before he looked back down at his sketch.

"I'd like to go next," a younger woman said. By now Louisa knew her name was Claire and that she'd lost both her parents in a tragic fire while she was away at school. She seemed a sweet and sincere person. "I found myself obsessing over that crack. I couldn't take my eyes off of it." She held up her drawing, which was rather interesting—one side was light and the other was dark. "I wanted to get the crack right. As I was working on it, I decided that it was kind of like my life."

"How is that?" Louisa asked.

"The crack runs right down the middle. Like my life was cut right down the middle when my parents died. Like this was my life before I lost them." She pointed to the lighter side of the drawing. "And that was my life after." She pointed to the darker side.

"I actually like the shaded side better," Louisa said honestly.

Claire nodded with a slight frown. "I sort of do too."

"It looks more real," someone else said.

They continued around the table, listening as each artist shared their work and their experience. They were barely finished when Louisa realized that the two-hour class had gone overtime.

"That was really good," she told everyone. "I feel like we all learned something valuable today." She smiled with satisfaction. "And, just think, this was only our first class."

"Will we meet again next week?" Bruce asked eagerly.

"We will," Louisa assured him. "But not the following week because of Christmas. Although I'd like to meet the week *after* Christmas if everyone wants to. I have a feeling I'll need it by then." To her relief, they all seemed eager to meet as often as possible. As they packed up their things, Louisa felt that, despite her shaky start, she might be able to manage this class after all. And perhaps in time she would actually understand the real workings of art therapy—or else she'd keep making it up as she went along.

It wasn't until Grace was driving through town, coming home late from work on Thursday, that she remembered she'd offered to host the angels' meeting tonight. One week ago, she had been all excited about having it at her house, thinking she'd have her Christmas decorations up and even some baking done. She'd even imagined preparing some small gift—something like Abby had done—to give to each of her friends.

But in reality, not a single decoration was up, she hadn't baked in ages, and her house needed to be cleaned. She glanced at her dashboard clock, deciding she had enough time to stop by the Harvester Bakery. Of course, when she got there, after parking across the street and running through the rain, she discovered they had just closed. Seeing someone inside, she even banged on the front door. But the woman scowled at her and disappeared into the back.

Soggy and cold, Grace continued driving home, hoping that she might have a package of store-bought cookies in her pantry. As soon as she parked in the garage, she dashed into the house, hoping that she could wrangle Joel into helping her do a whirl-wind cleaning. "The angels are coming tonight," she yelled at him as she ripped off her damp coat. "I need your help."

"*What?*" He looked at her like she'd lost her mind.

"The book group. They're meeting here." She started grabbing dishes out of the sink. "Why can't you ever put a dirty dish in the dishwasher?" she growled as she shoved a grimy plate in without bothering to rinse.

"Hello and good evening to you too," he said in an offended tone.

"I need you to help me clean up. After all, this is *your* mess."

"*My* mess?" He rolled his eyes. "Then let's leave it where it is. I *like* my mess."

"*Joel!*" she growled. "Help me *now*! They'll be here in about fifteen minutes."

"Why not let your friends see how we really live?" Joel taunted her. "Show them that you're not as perfect as you pretend to be."

She held a coffee mug in the air, ready to hurl it at him, then realized she'd simply have to clean up the broken shards. "Get out of here," she yelled angrily. "Go hide in your stupid man cave!"

He simply shrugged, then made himself scarce while she continued throwing the dishes into the dishwasher, knowing she'd need to rinse and rearrange them later. She put on the teakettle and started a pot of decaf, and while the coffee was brewing she wiped the kitchen counters. In the pantry, she dug around until she unearthed two packages of cookies, which she quickly arranged on a pretty plate before setting out cups and napkins.

It was a meager offering compared to Louisa's spread last week, but it would have to do. She was lighting a vanilla candle to set by the cookies when she heard the doorbell. Though she paused to smooth her hair and compose herself, she knew it was useless. Everything in her wanted to scream—she was not an angel and she never would be! Instead, she went to greet her guests. As she passed through the living room, she heard a crackling sound and was surprised to see that the fireplace was glowing warmly.

Joel had built a fire—and she had bit his head off.

Feeling like a heel, she opened the door to see that it was Belinda. "Right on time," Grace said a bit briskly. "Come in."

"Am I too early?" Belinda asked apologetically as she came into the foyer, peeling off a damp leather jacket. "I came directly from work."

"No, you're fine," Grace said as she hung up the jacket. "I'm the one who's running late. I totally forgot about tonight—until I was almost home. I guess I'm a little rattled."

"Sorry about that. Is there anything I can do to help?" Belinda sounded genuinely concerned.

Grace heard the teakettle whistling. "Come get yourself something warm to drink. Isn't it miserable out there?"

"Yes. I wish it would snow instead of rain." As Belinda poured a cup of decaf, Grace filled the creamer and set out some sugar.

"I've had a rotten week," Grace confessed as she made herself a cup of tea.

"I'm sorry." Belinda peered curiously at her. "I always imagine that your life is sweet perfection, so organized that you've got everything running like clockwork."

Grace laughed. "I'm sure I try to make it seem that way. But really, I think I'm losing it. More than ever now that Abby is gone. I can't believe how much I miss her."

"Me too." Belinda put a hand on her shoulder. "Is there anything I can do to help?"

Grace realized this was the second time Belinda had said

this—as if she really meant it, not like she was merely being polite. "I—uh—I don't know." Grace felt a lump in her throat. "Sometimes I think I just need someone to listen to me. A sympathetic ear, you know? Abby was like that."

"Well, here I am. All ears." Belinda sat on one of the stools by the island with an expectant expression.

Grace stared at Belinda, wondering if she could really open up to her the way she used to with Abby, but before she could make up her mind, the doorbell rang again.

"Maybe we should schedule a coffee date," Belinda said as she stood. "Let me get the door for you, Grace."

As Belinda went for the door, Grace attempted to compose herself once again. Somehow she needed to get through this evening without breaking into tears. It wouldn't be easy. She could hear that both Cassidy and Louisa had arrived now. Soon they had gotten their hot drinks and were seated in the living room where the crackling fire was surprisingly comforting. Grace would have to thank Joel . . . and apologize.

"I've had the most incredible week," Louisa began in a cheerful tone. She sounded happier than she had in more than a year—since losing Adam. She began to tell them about starting an art therapy class and how great it had turned out.

"I honestly didn't know what I was doing," Louisa confessed. "And at the beginning it was not going well at all. I was so embarrassed, I was ready to bolt and run. But then I prayed." She chuckled. "It was a pathetic and desperate prayer—but it was heartfelt. And then it all started to turn around. It was truly amazing. Almost miraculous."

"That's so cool," Cassidy exclaimed, and then she started to tell them about her idea to offer veterinary care to shut-ins. "I'm making house calls," she said eagerly. "Mostly to elderly people who are barely getting by. They all live in the same low-income housing. A sweet old lady named Dorothy Morgan keeps finding them for me. I've mostly been doing vaccinations and well-being checks. But the people are so appreciative. It's really fun. I wish I could do it full-time."

"So you're doing this for free?" Belinda asked with interest.

Cassidy nodded, then sipped her tea.

"That's so generous," Belinda told her.

"The pet owners are so grateful—yet I feel like I'm getting more out of it than they are. But they really do love their pets. And veterinary care is too expensive for their fixed-income budgets."

"And who pays for the vaccines and such?" Louisa asked with a concerned look.

"I do." Cassidy smiled. "I found a good, reputable website, and I've started ordering supplies online."

"But how can you afford that?" Louisa asked. "Especially when you're only working half-time?"

"I'm an angel," Cassidy said in a teasing tone. "The good Lord provides, right?"

"But you don't want to deplete your own finances," Belinda said gently. "You're a single woman, so you need to watch out for yourself."

Cassidy smiled brightly. "Don't worry, I'm being careful." She pointed back at Belinda. "How about you? What sort of angelic project have you taken on?"

Belinda grinned. "I was hoping you'd ask." She told them about the exciting fashion show project she was putting together with the new principal at McKinley High. "It was actually his idea to get these girls some fashion help," she explained. "Their clothing was . . . well, as Emma would say, it was pretty skanky."

Everyone laughed.

"Anyway, the girls met with me and really got on board.

Savannah and I have been putting together outfits, and the tickets are selling and, well, it's been going really well."

"It sounds like fun," Louisa said.

"It's been surprisingly fun," Belinda said happily. "Oh, sure, it's work too. But it feels so good to be helping these girls. I've been having them come in for their fittings separately. Only four so far. But it gives me a chance to talk to them one-on-one." She sighed. "Some of them come from some pretty troubled homes. It's no wonder they don't care about their appearance. And they're so hungry for positive attention." She looked hopefully at the group. "Which reminds me, I was hoping I could get some of you to help."

"How?" Louisa asked.

"At the fashion show. It's the Saturday before Christmas in the Amber Room. Anyway, it'll be kind of crazy behind the scenes. And I realize the whole thing could fall completely apart and turn into a disaster. So I could use a few more assistants. Helping the girls into the outfits and with their hair and makeup, and to keep everything moving smoothly, you know?"

Louisa and Cassidy both offered to help, but Grace simply sat there, saying nothing and feeling painfully close to tears. "I'd offer to help too," she blurted, "but I'm so—so overwhelmed—I'm not even sure I can do the project I agreed to do." The dam broke and she started to cry. The others gathered around her on the sectional, trying to comfort her and encouraging her to tell them what was wrong.

Finally, after blowing her nose, she explained about agreeing to decorate the living rooms of three Habitat homes. "But I thought they meant I was supposed to decorate them for Christmas—you know, put up a tree and some lights and greens and stuff. I didn't realize I was expected to fill three living rooms with donated furnishings and décor! I've spent the last four days calling all over and driving around town, trying to solicit donations. But it's not coming together. *Not at all.* Furniture stores are being really stingy and tight. Some are offering discounts, but I can't afford to purchase everything myself. And it is turning into—it's a big fat mess." She started to cry again.

"Is there some way we can help you?" Cassidy asked her.

"I—I don't really know how," Grace stammered. "Unless you know someone who wants to donate furniture pieces. Enough for three rooms."

The room got quiet.

"How about if we pray for you," Louisa said gently. "Since we're trying to be angels, it seems appropriate."

"That's what Abby would do," Cassidy added.

"That's right," Belinda agreed.

Grace wasn't sure that would make any difference, but simply nodded and bowed her head, waiting as each of them quietly said a short prayer for her. "Amen," Louisa said when they finished. "And now, as my mother used to say, let's add some legs to our prayers."

"How's that?" Grace asked.

"Well, I have some things I can donate. I stored some items in our attic, nice pieces, but they didn't really fit into our new home. I convinced myself that Matthew and Leah would want them eventually. Of course, they didn't. Anyway, I'd be happy to let you have them for your project if you like."

"Thank you!" Grace exclaimed.

"Hey, I've got a bunch of stuff in storage," Cassidy said suddenly. "It's so ridiculous paying for the storage unit every month. But I didn't know what to do with everything. It was from when my mom died . . . you know."

"And you really don't want it?" Grace asked hopefully.

"I'm sure there are mementos that I'll want to hold on to,"

Cassidy clarified. "Antiques and a few odds and ends. But not the furnishings. I mean they're nice and everything, but they're pretty traditional. Not my style. It was Abby's idea to put it all in there and deal with it later. But later never came. And I keep shelling out the monthly payments." She brightened. "That's money I could be using for pet meds."

"Well, I won't say no to anything," Grace told them. "And maybe I could help you sort through the unit for your own place. Help you figure out what you could use in your condo to make it more your style."

"That'd be great."

"And I have a few things too," Belinda told her. "You know me and flea markets. I'm there to look for clothes and I often come home with other things I don't need. Can't resist a bargain." She laughed. "You should see my storage room in the back of the shop. Stuff I thought I'd use to decorate. But mostly it gathers dust and gets in the way."

"I will gladly take anything you guys have to offer," Grace said gratefully. "And then I'll hope and pray I can arrange it all into three livable designs." But as Grace imagined the odds and ends she'd manage to collect from her friends, combined with the few items she'd already had donated, all she could envision was a mishmash of varying styles of cast-off furnishings that would probably be classified as "early garage sale."

At least the new homeowners would have something to sit on. Or so she hoped. As far as her reputation as a designer, well, there was no point fretting over that. When it was all said and done, Grace Westland would look like a complete failure—and maybe she deserved it. At least everyone would know the truth—that she was a fraud.

10

Grace arranged to go to Louisa's house first thing on Friday morning. Ironically, Louisa was donating some of the same pieces that Grace had felt were wrong for their new house back when she'd done the interior design nearly ten years ago. "I feel guilty," she confessed after she'd marked the pieces to be removed from the attic.

"Whatever for?" Louisa demanded. "I'm glad to be rid of these things."

"Because they're nice pieces, but I'm the one who discouraged you from using them in this house."

Louisa just laughed. "Don't forget that I'm the one who hired you. I wanted a fresh interior design for our new house—and I loved what you did for us." She set one of the table lamps on an end table. "I had no idea our economy was going to tank shortly thereafter."

"Well, thank you for your donation." She handed Louisa one of the tax-deductible receipts that Habitat had given her. "I'm sure it will be appreciated." As they went back downstairs,

Grace told her about the other family she'd met. "It was a couple in their sixties with an adult daughter with Down syndrome. Really sweet people and so happy to own their first home."

"Their first home in their sixties?" Louisa shook her head. "I guess we can be thankful."

"Yes, I've been thinking similar thoughts." Grace sighed. "Anyway, my moving guys should be around this afternoon with a truck to pick up the furniture. Is that okay?"

"I'll be here all day." Louisa smiled. "I'm actually working on a painting."

"Really? You're painting again?"

Louisa nodded eagerly. "Would you like to see it?"

"I'd love to."

Louisa led Grace into her painting studio, where Grace admired the beginnings of a winter farm scene. "It's beautiful, Louisa. You haven't lost your touch." She glanced around the studio, where various works were leaning against the walls and cabinets. "What are your plans for these other paintings? Are you going to have a showing someday?"

Louisa laughed. "Hardly. Those are my rejects."

"Rejects?" Grace picked up a still life, a mason jar of sunflowers, and studied it. "I could put this to use in a Habitat house."

"Then take it," Louisa told her. "Take any of them."

Feeling like she'd struck the mother lode, Grace selected several that she knew would be assets. "I'll get them framed and they will be lovely."

"Glad to help." Louisa winked. "Makes more room for me to create and store my new masterpieces."

⟶≫⟩⟩•◦◦•⟨⟨≪⟵

Cassidy met Grace at her storage unit after she finished work shortly after noon. She would've rather been making a house call right now, but she knew that emptying this unit would be worth the time it would take. Hopefully not more than a few hours.

"I haven't looked inside here for years," she confessed as she raised the door. "Might be infested with rats by now."

"According to the sign in front, this place is rodent-free," Grace pointed out.

"Right." Cassidy flicked on the light switch and, gazing over the piles of stuff, immediately felt overwhelmed. "Where do we begin?"

"Right here." Grace started moving things, making a pathway through the center. "I'm glad it's not raining today. We can set stuff out there. Then we'll load anything you're certain you don't want into the moving van and I'll sort it out later. Some will go in the new houses and some will be donated to Habitat Restore. Okay?"

"Works for me." Cassidy went over to an old trunk that, according to her mom, had been in the family for generations. "I'll definitely want to keep this." She removed a box from on top of it. "I think it might even look good in my condo."

"Progress!" Grace declared.

As the two of them worked together, sifting and sorting and hauling pieces into the back of the moving van, they talked. It wasn't long until Cassidy found herself confessing to Grace the sort of things she normally reserved for Abby.

"You are *not* fat!" Grace declared after they'd shoved a hutch into the van. "I don't want to hear you say that again, Cassidy. You're just a sturdily built girl. And look how strong you are. I never could've gotten that in there without you."

"Well, guys like skinny chicks," Cassidy said as she wiped her hands on the back of her jeans.

"That is not true." Grace firmly shook her head. "I was a skinny chick when I married Joel, and he confessed that he liked it better when I put on some weight after having the twins. And I know he was being honest. Besides, I've read surveys where the majority of guys say they prefer curvy girls over skinny ones. So don't believe that old lie."

Cassidy frowned. "But Dorothy Morgan—that's one of my house-call clients and a good friend—invited me over to meet her grandson tonight, and she's been talking me up to him like I'm some kind of prize. He's probably expecting some blonde bombshell and—"

"Stop putting yourself down, Cass."

"I know . . . it's dumb. But old habits are hard to break."

"You have so much to offer a guy. You're smart and funny and kind. You've got an education and a career." She tweaked Cassidy's ponytail. "And if you fixed yourself up a little, you could really turn his head."

"You sound exactly like Abby."

"Thank you." Grace smiled triumphantly.

By the time they were done, only a couple hours later, Cassidy was relieved to have emptied the storage unit—but even more than that, she was happy to have made a real friend. She and Grace had been friendly acquaintances before, but they'd never been close. Not like she'd felt today. This was something new—and it felt good.

Belinda had finished her last after-school fitting with a high school girl when Cassidy burst into her shop. "You gotta help me," Cassidy said with tear-filled eyes.

"What on earth is it?" Belinda demanded as she laid down her notebook.

Cassidy held out a wrinkled white bundle. "The cats killed her."

"Killed *who*?" Belinda stared at her in horror.

"My angel. I don't know how it happened, but sometimes the cats get pretty crazy when I'm gone. Anyway, when I got home after emptying my storage unit with Grace, I found *this*."

Belinda peeled back the tissue paper to see mangled pieces of lace, ribbon, and fabric—what was left of Cassidy's angel ornament. "Oh, Cassidy, I'm so sorry."

"Can you fix her? You're the best seamstress I know. You've got to put her back together."

Belinda laid the pieces on the countertop, starting to rearrange them and seeing some pieces were missing. Probably ingested by Cassidy's devilish felines. "I think so." She made a sad smile. "You'll have to leave the patient with me overnight though." As she fiddled with what was left of the angel, she touched something stiff underneath the angel's tattered dress. It felt like a small roll of paper. Out of curiosity, she removed the tiny scroll, seeing it was tied with a thin gold thread. "Look." She held it out to Cassidy. "Looks like something's printed on it."

Cassidy unrolled the miniature scroll, studying it carefully before she read the words aloud. "'I praise you, for I am fearfully and wonderfully made. Wonderful are your works; my soul knows it very well.' Psalm 139:14." She looked up at Belinda. "Wow, that's pretty cool."

"Abby must've put that there for you, Cassidy. Like a secret message."

"Yeah." Cassidy continued to stare down at the words. "I like that verse."

"Do you believe what it says?" Belinda asked gently. "That God made *you*, that he made you *wonderfully*?"

Cassidy looked up with misty eyes. "To be honest, I'm not so sure. I'd like to believe it." She sighed. "It's ironic. Only this afternoon Grace lectured me about something like this. She said to stop putting myself down."

"Grace said that?" Belinda was surprised.

"Yeah. It was kind of like listening to Abby."

"Well, good for Grace." Belinda honed in on Cassidy's appearance now. As usual, she had on her veterinary scrubs, and her hair was pulled back in a tight ponytail. "I'm really into makeovers these days," Belinda said lightly. "You know, for the upcoming fashion show."

"Uh-huh?"

"How about I give you one?" Belinda made a hopeful smile.

"*Me?*" Cassidy blinked. "You want *me* in your fashion show?"

"Well, that wasn't what I meant. But if you wanted to—"

"No way!"

"Fine. I meant a plain old makeover. Just for the fun of it." Belinda grabbed Cassidy by the hand, calling out to Savannah. "We'll be in the back room—watch the shop." She led Cassidy back to the station she'd set up for the fashion show fittings, complete with its dressing table, makeup samples, hair tools, and accessories, as well as a few other goodies. "You take down that ponytail and I'll be back in a few minutes."

Without waiting to hear protests, Belinda dashed out to speak to Savannah, explaining her impromptu plan and estimating Cassidy's clothing sizes. "You gather up a casual but stylish outfit that you think might work for a blue-eyed blonde. Keep in mind she's a no-frills, low-maintenance sort of girl. Do your best and bring it back to me ASAP."

Savannah grinned like she was eager for a new fashion challenge. As she headed for the racks, Belinda scurried back to start work on Cassidy, hoping her frowsy friend hadn't made a quick escape out the back door.

"What are you going to do?" Cassidy asked nervously, shaking her long hair out.

"Something Abby had been wanting to do for ages."

"Oh." Cassidy frowned.

"Trust me, Cass."

Cassidy's shoulders relaxed a bit as she leaned back in the chair. "Okay . . ."

As Belinda brushed out her thick hair, she explained what she felt it needed, but when she pulled out her scissors and comb, Cassidy looked genuinely frightened. "I used to be a hairdresser," Belinda confessed. "I'm not licensed now, but I'm not charging you either, so it's okay. I promise."

"What are you going to do?" Cassidy asked for the second time.

"I want to feather in some bangs and some gentle wisps along the sides to soften it up. Maybe a bit of layering since your hair's so thick. But don't worry, I'm leaving the length in the body of it. I know you're a ponytail girl and you can still do that, but, honestly, you need to let this gorgeous hair down sometimes. Really, you've got such beautiful hair, Cass. Thick and healthy. And do you know how rare natural blondes are? Anyway, we want to soften it up—make it frame your face."

"Okay," Cassidy agreed with uncertainty.

And then, turning Cass away from the mirror the same way she'd done with the high school girls, Belinda started to snip. "I quit doing hair when I was pregnant with Emma. It was hard on my body being on my feet all day. My shoulders and back would ache like the devil by evening. That's when I started planning for my resale shop." Belinda rambled about her early years as a retailer, snipping here and there until she was satisfied.

"Can I look?"

"Not yet." Belinda reached for the makeup samples. They were from a line that she carried in her shop, quality products albeit a little pricey. "The makeover isn't finished. And don't worry, I'm giving you a soft, natural look," she assured

Cassidy as she brushed on some soft pink blush. "Playing up your great features. You have beautiful eyes. And that mouth." She smacked her own lips. "Well, you can thank the good Lord for those nice full lips. White girls usually don't come by lips like that naturally."

Cassidy giggled.

"Here you go," Savannah announced as she entered the back room with an armful of clothes, hanging them one by one on the nearby rack. "I got a variety of sizes and styles, to give you something to pick from."

Belinda glanced at the rack of garments. "Those look great. Thanks!"

Before long, Cassidy's makeover was complete. Her hair gently framed her face. Her makeup, though light and casual, brought out her natural beauty. And the outfit they finally decided on—a great pair of jeans, a boho-chic top, and a nicely worn denim jacket, plus accessories—was very stylish. In fact, the girl looked hot. Honestly, the transformation was nothing short of miraculous.

"Wow!" Belinda stared at her protégé. "Is that really you?"

"Let me see." Cassidy turned to peer into the full-length mirror, blinking in surprise. "Wow is right. *How did you do that?*"

"I had the right stuff to work with." Belinda put an arm around Cassidy's shoulders. "Meaning you, sweetheart. You're gorgeous. And don't you forget it!"

"Wow." Cassidy reached for her wallet, insisting on paying Belinda for the clothes.

"Put that money toward more pet vaccines. My contribution." Belinda picked up the curled piece of paper from the dressing table. "You hold on to this verse, Cass. In your heart as well as in your hand. And I'll repair your angel and get her back to you."

Cassidy threw her arms around Belinda. "Thanks so much!"

"Thanks for letting me do it." Belinda pointed upward. "I just wish Abby could look down to see you right now."

"Who knows?" Cassidy made a funny smile. "And did I even tell you what I'm doing tonight?"

"No. Something special?"

"Well, probably not. It's only dinner with my old lady friend Dorothy Morgan."

Belinda tried to hide her disappointment. "You'll look nice anyway."

"Dorothy's grandson is supposed to stop by." Cassidy smirked. "Dorothy's been wanting me to meet him."

Belinda laughed as she realized the timeliness of this makeover. "You better let me know how it goes." She walked Cassidy through the shop. "I want a full report when I give you your angel back."

"You were my angel today," Cassidy said happily. "Thanks for everything!"

<hr />

By the end of the workday Grace felt like she'd made real progress. Between Louisa and Cassidy, she had quite an interesting selection of furnishings. Not anything she'd ever have used in a "real" design, but they were sturdy and serviceable. What more could she hope for? Plus, she hadn't even seen what Belinda had to offer yet. That would come tomorrow. Hopefully it would add some spice to these meat and potatoes selections.

As she walked through the storage room in the back of her design shop, she knew she wasn't there yet. But somehow she had to make it work. Somehow she had to transform these miscellaneous pieces into three attractive rooms. Okay, scratch attractive—at this stage, she would settle for functional. Functional with a tiny bit of style.

As she perused and measured and made notes for the various houses, she thought about when Louisa had insisted upon praying for Grace's challenge. And now, less than twenty-four hours later, it really was starting to fall into place. Like a little miracle. Even if she had a long distance to run before she could celebrate.

She also knew that she needed to make things up with Joel. Or at least try. They hadn't exchanged a single word since her blowup last night. She'd considered texting him "I'm sorry," but it sounded flat and phony. She'd rather say it in person tonight.

But first she'd promised to stop by the third Habitat house to introduce herself to the family who would occupy it. They were the only ones she had yet to meet and, as a designer, she knew not to underestimate the value of the physical connection. She needed to get a feel for this family, to determine who they were and what mattered to them. Not that she could deliver it. But she could at least try.

When she got to the house, she saw a slightly beat-up blue minivan in the driveway and figured it belonged to the new owners. All she knew was that they were a family of four and that they had military connections.

As with the other families, Grace was prepared for another hard-luck story, but when she saw the beautiful young woman in the wheelchair she was taken aback. "Hello," the woman said cheerfully. "Come in."

Grace quickly introduced herself, explaining why she was here.

"I'm Amy," the woman said pleasantly. "My husband, Josh, and the twins are out back, making plans for some sort of play yard or fort or something—I'm not really sure what he has in mind."

"You have twins?" Grace stammered, trying not to stare at the place where Amy's legs should've been.

"Yes. Caleb and Callie. They're seven and a half—and a handful."

"I can imagine." Grace forced a smile. "I mean, I really can. I have twins too. A boy and girl, just like yours. But they're nearly twenty now. And to be honest, they're still a handful."

Amy laughed. "Well, that's not very encouraging."

"True. But seven is a delightful age," Grace said quickly. "They might even still believe in Santa Claus, right?"

Amy looked down at her lap. "I don't know about that. When I came home . . . well, looking like this . . . I think they started to question a lot of things."

"Amy!" a man called, followed by children's excited voices. "There's tons of space. Plenty of room in the yard for—" He stopped, seeing Grace. "Sorry. I didn't know anyone else was here."

Following more introductions, Josh explained about how he'd been trying to get their family into a Habitat house ever since Amy had been assigned overseas. And how it had all come together last summer. "But we never expected our home to be furnished," he told her. "Not that we're complaining. We couldn't be happier about it. The kids and I had been living with my mom while Amy was serving overseas, so we really didn't have much in the way of furniture. We really appreciate what you folks are doing. This will be our best Christmas ever." He put a hand on Amy's shoulder. "All of us back together again—in our own home."

"Well, I only came by to say hello and get a feel for what sort of things you guys might like." She made an uneasy smile. "Not that we have a lot to choose from, since the plan is already sort of in place." She didn't want to admit that her plan was to make the best use of castoffs from friends. "But what kind of things do you guys like? What sort of style and color and whatnot?"

"We don't really care," Amy told her. "Mostly we want to be together—and to be comfortable. We'll probably love whatever you do."

"And this house has been built specially, to accommodate Amy's needs," Josh explained. "With wide hallways and doorways and that ramp you saw out front."

"Until I get my prostheses," Amy clarified. "Hopefully I won't need it after that. But that might not be for another year or so. There's quite a waiting list."

Grace nodded. "And favorite colors?" she asked Amy.

"Blue," Amy told her. "But to be honest, I'm not sure I want a bunch of blue in the house. Unless it's a nice soft aqua blue. That'd be nice."

Grace made a note of this, then asked a few more questions. Amy expressed a fondness for contemporary style, and Josh said he wanted a big-screen TV. Longing for a Santa Claus she could take this list to, Grace jotted their thoughts down. She knew the chance of having this room meet their expectations would be slim. But what else could she do?

Finally, saying she needed to get home, she bid them good night and hurried on out. As she drove home, she wished there was a way to give them all they wanted. Really, in the big scheme of things, it was small. As she pulled up to her house, she felt painfully aware of even more things that she needed to be thankful for. Legs, for instance.

As she closed the garage door, she remembered her need to apologize to Joel. But seeing that his car wasn't in the garage, she could only hope that he hadn't gotten home yet. And perhaps that was a good thing.

She carried the bag of groceries that she'd picked up on her way home into the kitchen. Her plan was to make a nice consolation dinner—and to apologize profusely. But first she went into the living room to make a fire in the fireplace. She wanted everything to be cozy and perfect by the time Joel got home. Especially since he'd made her a fire last night.

It felt good to be puttering around the kitchen. By 6:30 she had the table nicely set, candles lit, the makings of a good dinner in the oven, and even a few appetizers out on the island. Not to mention that the fire in the living room was crackling cheerfully. The stage was all set for her to eat crow. But where was Joel?

By 7:30 the dinner was done and being kept warm in the oven, but despite several texts, she still hadn't heard back from her MIA husband. Worried that something might've happened to him, she finally decided to call.

"I told you last week that it was the office Christmas party tonight," he said with a tinge of impatience. "Remember, you told me you didn't want to come?"

"Oh, yeah." She sank onto the living room sectional. "I totally forgot. I just wanted to make sure you're okay. Sorry to bother you."

"Sorry you're not here," he said unconvincingly. "It's a great party. Good food and good music. And they're playing some goofy games with some nice prizes too."

"Have fun," she said in a slightly choked voice. "See you later." Then she hung up and—longing for something, yet not even sure what—she sat there and cried.

11

Cassidy knew it was silly to feel so nervous. After all, she was simply having dinner with Dorothy Morgan. Maybe Dorothy's grandson would stop by to say hey and maybe he wouldn't. Dorothy hadn't even been completely sure. For all Cassidy knew, as she rang the doorbell, it might only be her and the old lady and the cat. And that would be fine.

"Come in, come in," Dorothy said warmly. "Don't you look nice! I've never seen you with your hair down, Cassidy. So very pretty. Here, let me take your overcoat."

Cassidy peeled off her parka, handing it over.

"Brent is busy in the kitchen. He's helping me with dinner. Did I mention that my grandson is a fabulous cook?"

Cassidy tried to hide her surprise—not that Brent was cooking dinner, but that he'd actually shown up. As Dorothy chattered at her, giving an update on Buster the dog's improved coat, Cassidy suddenly envisioned Brent as short, bald, and middle-aged, rudely talking down to her and picking his teeth at the table. Okay, she knew she was being extreme and juvenile, not to mention shallow, but she was determined not to get her hopes up. If Brent did turn out to be disappointing, at least she'd be prepared.

"Hello?" a male voice called from the kitchen. Cassidy turned to see a lanky guy with curly dark hair grinning at her. "You made it."

As Dorothy conducted a proper introduction, Cassidy tried not to gape at the good-looking man shaking her hand. "You like my apron?" He grinned as he waved down at the flowery garment. "Grandma insisted."

"To protect your nice shirt," Dorothy said as she untied it from behind him. "Brent is a good cook, but messy—oh my!"

"And the marinara sauce was splattering." He smiled at Cassidy. "I hope you like Italian."

"I love Italian."

"And you're not vegan or dairy or wheat intolerant, are you?"

"Nope. No allergies, no restrictions."

"Cool. When Grandma told me you're a veterinarian, I misheard her and thought she'd said *vegetarian*." He chuckled. "That could be problematic with my famous meatballs."

"I love meatballs." Cassidy couldn't help but like this guy. "But I can't believe you're doing the cooking. That's so nice of you."

"Well, consider this my way of thanking you for helping Grandma with her cat. She told me what you did for Muffin—and how you're helping her neighbors—and I thought, I gotta meet this girl."

Dorothy grinned triumphantly. "Didn't I tell you he was a nice boy?" she gently nudged Cassidy with her elbow.

"Everything's almost done," he told Dorothy. "Maybe you ladies can finish setting the table."

Cassidy felt her hopes rising, but as she set the table, she reminded herself that this could still go sideways. It wouldn't be the first time either. Just in case, Cassidy was determined to play her hand carefully. Sure, she thought Brent was good-looking and interesting and just plain fun. But she also knew that she'd scared off more than one guy with her unbridled enthusiasm before. *Play it cool*, she told herself as they eventually sat down together at the little dinette table.

As before, Dorothy said a nice blessing, and then, as they ate, the conversation seemed to flow normally and naturally. Cassidy felt herself relaxing until she was almost at ease. That was a first—at least when she was out with an attractive guy. But of course, she reminded herself, this wasn't a date.

"So you work at Auberon Animal Hospital?" Brent asked as he reached for the salad bowl.

"Yes. I felt really fortunate to get hired there right after college. That was almost five years ago, but I'm still only working half-time."

"I don't understand that," Dorothy said. "A fine veterinarian like you and they only let you work half time? Doesn't seem fair to me."

"But that does give you time to make your house calls, right?" Brent said.

Cassidy nodded as she spooned some dressing on her salad. "In fact, it's made me start rethinking my whole career."

"You wouldn't quit being a veterinarian, would you?" he asked with concern.

"No, I love being a vet. I love animals. But I think there might be a need for mobile veterinarians in this town. I've been wondering about getting a van and equipping it like a mobile clinic—maybe even with a surgical unit. Not for real serious operations, maybe things like spaying and neutering and simple procedures. I'd probably need to have sterile kennel units for pet owners to use during their pet's recovery. I haven't worked out all the details yet, but I think I could provide a valuable service. With less overhead, I wouldn't have to charge people as much. And I think it would be less stressful on the animals to recover in their own homes."

"That's a fabulous idea." Brent buttered a roll.

"I think so too," Dorothy agreed. "I have to admit that I felt very distressed to think my poor Muffin had to spend a night at the veterinarian. I worried that she'd be upset about it. But what could I do?"

"Sometimes, when animals are severely ill or medicated, they don't appear overly aware of their surroundings," Cassidy assured her. "But some animals can become quite stressed in a strange place."

"Well, of course," Dorothy said. "Animals are not so different than people. They know their owners and their homes. It stands to reason that they would get well quicker in a familiar place."

"That's exactly what I'm thinking," Cassidy confirmed.

"You know, I read an article about a woman who claimed she could talk to the animals," Brent said. "Kind of like a dog whisperer. Anyway, she talked about how a lot of pets would become very disturbed about going to the veterinarian. She said they were confused and frightened by it." He laughed. "Apparently they told her."

"I actually read that woman's book in college," Cassidy said eagerly. "Even though I thought she was a little whacky, she did make some good points. It's helped me to be more empathetic. Don't get me wrong, I really respect my boss's experience. Dr. Auberon has been practicing veterinary medicine for longer than I've been alive. But he's a little old-school. He's always accusing me of coddling the animals."

"Good grief, I should think he would appreciate that," Dorothy said.

"If I had a pet, I'd want to take it to a veterinarian with compassion," Brent assured her.

"Me too," Cassidy said. "That's why I try to empathize with how our pet patients might feel. I mean, imagine you're a cat or dog and your owner takes you to the vet. Everything looks and smells different. Your beloved owner leaves you there by yourself. And suddenly you've got strangers who poke you and prod you and lock you in a little cage. Then you hear other frightened animals howling and whining all night long. Wouldn't it be terrifying?"

"Sounds kind of like a bad sci-fi movie." Brent chuckled. "One where you're abducted by aliens and held captive inside a flying saucer while the aliens experiment on you."

"Exactly," she said. "That's a good analogy of how it might feel to a pet being treated at the vet clinic."

"Oh my." Dorothy frowned. "Perhaps that was another reason I never wanted to take poor Muffin to the veterinarian."

"Don't get me wrong," Cassidy clarified. "There are lots of situations where a good vet clinic saves animals' lives. But there are lots of minor treatments that don't necessarily need all that."

"And there are folks who can't afford it," Dorothy reminded her.

They continued to talk about the mobile vet clinic, brainstorming together, coming up with various ideas for how it might work. Cassidy was thoroughly enjoying herself—and she was falling for Brent. But at least she wasn't showing it.

As she helped to clean up after the meal, Dorothy apologized for not having fixed a dessert. "I hoped that I could send you two kids out for ice cream." She winked at Cassidy, almost as if she had planned this from the start. "There's a really good shop just a few—"

"Sorry, Grandma." Brent leaned down and pecked Dorothy on the cheek. "I can't do that tonight."

"Oh?" Dorothy frowned. "You have other plans?"

"Something I need to take care of—before tomorrow." He hung up his dish towel. "So if you ladies will excuse me, I'm going to bail out even before the cleanup is done."

"No problem, I can finish up in here." Cassidy forced what she hoped looked like a genuine smile. "Thank you for making such a great dinner."

"Yes, thank you." Dorothy still looked troubled. "You really have to go home so early?"

He made an apologetic smile. "Sorry, but I do."

He told Cassidy that he'd been glad to meet her and, just like that, he grabbed his coat and left.

"I'm so sorry," Dorothy told Cassidy. "Brent is usually not that rude."

"That wasn't rude," Cassidy said lightly. "He just had somewhere he needed to be." She put a hand on Dorothy's shoulder, guiding her to the living room. "And I insist you go put your feet up while I finish up in here."

Dorothy started to protest, but Cassidy wouldn't allow it. Finally, with Dorothy in her recliner and *Jeopardy!* playing on the TV, Cassidy returned to the kitchen. As she continued cleaning up, she reminded herself that this was nothing new. She usually had that effect on guys. They would meet her and act cordial for a while, but before the evening ended, they would lose interest. She usually blamed herself for being too eager, but she didn't think she'd done that tonight.

Of course, she had monopolized the conversation. She hadn't really meant to, but both Brent and Dorothy had seemed so interested . . . and supportive. But perhaps they were simply being polite. And really, what difference did it make? This was how it always went with her. When it came to guys, she was useless. The sooner she accepted her fate to be the spinster cat lady, the better off she would be. You can't get your heart broken if you don't go throwing it out there for some guy to trample on. Still, she had really believed that Brent was different. Of course, she'd been wrong . . . again.

Grace had arranged to meet Belinda at her shop on Saturday, in order to see what she might be willing to donate to the Habitat project. The plan was to meet early, even before the shop opened, since Belinda hoped to have a busy day. Considering that the Christmas shoppers would be out and about following this morning's Christmas parade, it made sense. But it also meant that Grace got up while Joel, worn out from his late-night Christmas party, was still sleeping. Perhaps it was for the best, since she was still smoldering over being stood up—and her ruined dinner. She knew it was unreasonable on her part, but it was how she felt.

"I brought us coffees," Grace announced. She handed Belinda a latte that had been made exactly like Belinda liked it.

"You're an angel!" Belinda laughed as she sniffed it. "Oh, that's right, we all are."

"I don't feel much like an angel," Grace confessed as Belinda led her into the back room. "If you knew what I wanted to do to my husband last night—" She stopped herself, embarrassed that she'd said that much.

"What did you want to do to him?" Belinda's dark eyes twinkled with curiosity as she leaned against a cabinet, sipping her latte.

Grace waved a dismissive hand. "You know how it goes. He'd gotten my goat—I guess I wanted to drop-kick him over the goal post of life." She laughed. "No big deal."

"What happened?" Belinda gently prodded her. "I always thought of you two as being very close. Anyway, that was how Abby painted it. I remember how you and Joel vacationed with Abby and Clayton last year. From what I heard, Grace and Joel Westland were all sweetness and light."

Suddenly Grace found herself opening up, spilling about how she and Joel had been at odds with each other ever since they'd disagreed over the twins at Thanksgiving. "To be honest, it started even before that. But Thanksgiving was when it seemed to come to a head. Now it seems like all we do is argue," she said sadly. "Over anything and everything. And I realize that a lot of it is my fault. I've been stressed out over my angel project. I know I bit off more than I can chew. I didn't do it intentionally. And I would think that Joel would be more understanding—or even offer to help. But he hasn't."

"Maybe he thinks you're handling it fine on your own. And at least you've got your friends helping you. According to Cassidy, you're making progress." Belinda pointed to where a dressing table and mirror was set up in a corner, explaining how she'd given Cassidy a makeover yesterday. "I wanted to give her confidence a makeover too. Cass said you'd encouraged her along those same lines."

"I did." Grace nodded eagerly. "I'm so glad you did that. How did she look?"

"Really great. And she had a date last night. Well, she didn't call it a date. It was her old lady friend and her grandson. Anyway, when Cass left here, she was in good spirits." Belinda picked up an angel ornament. "Her cats had torn this up," she said as she twirled it on her finger.

"But it looks okay." Grace leaned forward to see better.

"That's because she's been in angel surgery." Belinda told Grace about the Bible verse that had been tied underneath the angel's lacy gown. "It was the verse about how we are fearfully and wonderfully made by God. I think it was Abby's way of nudging Cassidy to appreciate herself more."

"That's amazing. It's exactly what I told her yesterday," Grace declared.

"I think Abby might've put a verse in each of our angels."

"Seriously?"

"Yeah. I found mine last night."

"What did it say?"

"I don't have it with me, but as soon as I read it, I remembered it as a verse my grandmother used to say to me. It's Jeremiah 29:11, and it says that God knows the plans he has for me—that they're good plans that won't hurt me—and that I'll have hope and a good future." Belinda smiled.

"That's encouraging."

"I know."

Grace grimaced. "Maybe I need to go see if my angel has some secret message for me. She'll probably tell me to quit being so hard on my husband." She smirked at Belinda. "I had actually planned to apologize to Joel last night. I'd made this really nice dinner and had a fire going in the fireplace and everything. But he was off at his stupid office party—having too good a time to come home to his poor lonely wife. He didn't even get home until well past midnight."

"Why didn't you go to the party with him?"

Grace shrugged. "I don't know . . ." She actually did know. She had declined to go because she'd been angry when he'd told her about it. She had thought she could punish him by refusing to go. It seemed like she'd only punished herself, though.

"So, I'm curious, Grace, are your worst marital problems in regard to your kids and how they're wasting their college tuition? Did I understand you right?"

Grace nodded glumly.

"And Joel has never cheated on you?" Belinda's eyes narrowed slightly.

"No, of course not."

"And he's not an alcoholic or a gambler or an abuser or anything like that?" Belinda peered closely at Grace, clearly studying her.

"No, nothing like that." Grace frowned uncomfortably. "He's actually quite decent. On a good day, he's rather likeable."

"You want to know the truth?" Belinda sighed. "If my husband had been a little more like Joel—if he'd stuck around—I think I might still be married. And if he'd invited me to a Christmas party last night, I would've been there with bells on."

Grace started to cry now.

"I'm sorry." Belinda put a hand on her back. "I guess I shouldn't have said that. Abby was always warning me not to say everything that came into my head. As you can see, I'm still learning." She handed Grace a tissue.

As Grace blew her nose, she knew that Belinda wasn't trying to be mean. She was only being honest. Belinda's husband had cheated on her and he'd been abusive too. According to Abby, it had been a blessing in disguise when he'd abandoned Belinda shortly after Emma had been born. But that was more than twenty years ago. None of them could figure out why someone as beautiful and intelligent as Belinda had remained single all these years. Abby said it was because of Emma. Belinda had devoted herself to raising her.

If Grace hadn't felt like her own life was such a mess, she might've asked Belinda about this. As it was, she was barely able to keep her emotions together as they went through Belinda's back room, picking and choosing items that Grace felt would work for the Habitat homes.

"Thanks for all these great pieces," Grace told Belinda shortly before Glad Rags was supposed to open for business. "They will add some real personality to the rooms. I'll send my moving guys over on Monday to pick them up." Grace hugged Belinda. "And thanks for listening to me—and for saying what you said. In a way it reminded me of Abby."

"Really?" Belinda looked hopeful.

"It was like Abby—with sharp teeth."

Belinda grimaced.

"But I needed it."

"We're setting chairs out on the sidewalk to watch the parade." Belinda walked Grace to the front of the shop. "Want to join us?"

"Sounds fun, but I need to go to my studio and get to work. Thanks to my Habitat project, I'm way behind."

"That's too bad." Belinda sadly shook her head. "If you change your mind, you're welcome."

Grace thanked her again, but she knew she wouldn't be coming back. Not because it didn't sound fun but because, like she said, thanks to her angel project, her real work was getting neglected. She knew her paying clients would be understanding—at least during the holidays. But Christmas would come and go, and then they'd expect their design dreams to be put perfectly into place. One client, vacationing in Hawaii during December, expected her home remodel to be completely finished in time for her big New Year's Eve party. Grace didn't have time for parades or parties—she had work to do!

12

The design studio was dark and quiet as Grace let herself in the back door. Typical for a Saturday, and a big reason she often worked on weekends. With no distractions or interruptions, she could accomplish more than twice as much. She hurried up the stairs, turning on the lights in her loft studio and opening the blinds to let even more light in. She glanced down to Main Street below, where spectators were already gathering to watch the parade. It must be nice to have that kind of free time.

As she set her bag down on her big worktable, she noticed her angel ornament dangling from the desk lamp. She'd left it there to remind herself that the Habitat homes were her angel project. Not that she needed much reminding since she'd pretty much been thinking about it night and day lately. As she turned on her computer, she remembered what Belinda had said about the "secret message" that she and Cassidy had discovered. Was it possible that Abby had left an angel message for Grace as well?

Feeling anticipation akin to opening a Chinese fortune

cookie, Grace peeled back the layers of lace and satin and felt around on the angel. Sure enough, there was a tiny paper scroll. It was secured around the angel's midsection with a piece of gold thread. Grace removed the thread and unrolled the small scroll, longing for some words of encouragement. But all it said was "Matthew 6."

"Huh?" Grace stared down at the words. Did that mean she was supposed to read a whole chapter from the Bible? It wasn't that she was unwilling to read a whole chapter, but she felt slightly irked by it. Why had Abby given Belinda and Cassidy a few lines, but decided that Grace needed an entire chapter? She tossed the curly paper aside and turned her attention to the computer screen, but unable to focus now—thanks to that slip of paper—she knew she had to find out what that chapter said.

Grace went over to her bookshelf, where she was pretty certain she had a New Testament—one that Abby had given her for Christmas several years ago after Grace had confessed to never reading the Bible. Sure enough, the book was wedged between a design book and an old furniture catalog. She blew the dust off the Bible and opened it up, flipping a few pages until she came to the specified chapter.

She no longer felt the fortune-cookie anticipation. Instead, she felt aggravated. Really, she didn't have time for this! To read a *whole* chapter? What was Abby trying to say to her anyway? Grace decided she would simply read the first line or two, then skim a bit—and get back to what she should be doing—*working!*

She took in a deep breath and started to read. She could barely get past the first couple of sentences. It was a strong warning—*not to do good deeds publicly*. She laid the book down with an uneasy feeling gnawing inside of her. Wasn't that exactly what she'd done with the Habitat project? Doing her "good deeds" so everyone could see them? She'd acted like a spoiled show-off, going around town talking the project up—even complaining about what a hardship it was for her—like she was some sort of saint.

But according to this section of Scripture, she should be doing this work in private—so that only God could see her. Although these verses cut her to the core, they also resonated deep inside. It made sense, and she felt like she really should've known better.

At the same time, she reminded herself she wasn't completely mercenary. After all, she really had come to care about the new homeowners. Hadn't she gotten more interested in the project after meeting them? Hadn't her heartstrings been tugged? But the real truth was that she never would've agreed to help in the first place—not without the incentive of having her name attached to the project. She wanted the public relations and advertising—all good for her design firm. But now she understood that by continuing along her PR-motivated path, her only reward would be some cheap temporary publicity. Whereas if she did it secretly—simply because she wanted to help—God would be pleased with her.

She stared at the angel Abby had made her and, just like that, she knew what needed to happen. She would continue her Habitat project—wholeheartedly—and in such a way that no one would realize it was Grace Westland or her design firm that was responsible for it. She would leave no placards in the Habitat homes, she would discontinue boasting and complaining about it. She would do everything possible to remove her fingerprints from the whole thing.

Interestingly, as this realization hit her, she felt surprisingly free inside. Like a weight had been lifted. Suddenly now she wanted to read the rest of the Scripture Abby had given her.

So she continued to read, slowly taking in the words of what she decided must be the best chapter in the whole Bible. Why had she never read it before? In the middle of everything was the Lord's Prayer, something she knew from years of attending church, but seldom prayed with genuine sincerity.

She felt another jolt of reality as she read the verses reminding her that God was far more important than money. She knew this in her head . . . but in her heart? Not so much. In fact, this was exactly what had been coming between her and Joel of late. They'd been fighting over the expenses of the twins' tuition. Beating each other up and making each other miserable when they should've been trusting God instead. She wondered what Joel would think about these Scriptures.

Finally, she came to the end of the chapter. These warnings were in regard to worrying. This really hit home with her. So much of her life had become wrapped in worry during the past several years. It had started when she'd grown her design business from working out of her home to working downtown in her rather expensive studio. In fact, that was exactly why she was working today—simply because she was so anxious and worried about getting everything done on time. She stared at the verse that said not to worry about tomorrow—that each day had enough troubles of its own.

She shut the New Testament and closed her eyes. Could she even do that? Could she *stop* worrying? Could she trust God to take care of tomorrow? She knew what Abby would tell her right now—and that was what Grace did. She bowed her head and asked God to help her—she would need a lot of God's help in order to put these principles into practice. But she knew she wanted to—from the bottom of her heart she wanted to.

As she said "amen" she heard the shrill call of the fire engine siren signaling that the Christmas parade was starting up on the other end of town. She went over to the window, suddenly remembering the times she'd taken the twins to the parade when they were small, and later on when she and Joel would go to watch the kids participating in a school float or drill team or marching band.

"Why am I still up here?" she asked herself. "If I'm trusting God for tomorrow, shouldn't I be down there watching the Christmas parade today?" As minor as this decision would seem to anyone else, it felt like a very big deal to Grace. A big step in the right direction.

Grabbing her coat and scarf, she raced down the stairs and across the street to where Belinda and Savannah were already sitting in their camp chairs in front of Glad Rags with a thermos sitting between them.

"You decided to join us after all." Belinda dragged a spare camp chair over to set up next to hers.

"Have some cocoa." Savannah filled a cup, handing it to her.

Belinda pointed down the street to where the first float was coming. "You're just in time."

Grace sighed as she sniffed the cocoa. She was both just in time and a little late—but maybe she could start changing that now.

Belinda scheduled the dress rehearsal for the fashion show for Wednesday morning. With about a week until Christmas, everyone was busy—including her—and it was tempting to skip a rehearsal. But she knew these girls needed serious coaching. Besides, she reminded herself as she drove over to the high school, where she'd arranged to use the auditorium, this was bigger than simply a fashion show.

By now she felt like she'd established some pretty good relationships with most of the girls. And she knew, after hearing some of their family histories, that these girls needed role models in their lives. Not that she'd ever considered herself a role model before. But after Remmie tearfully thanked her for helping her, saying that Belinda was the first person to take time like that with her, Belinda realized how important this fund-raiser really was.

Because school had already let out for Christmas break, Belinda could park right in front. As she walked up to the school, she saw Carey striding out to meet her. "I've already unlocked the auditorium," he explained as he reached to carry the oversized bag she'd brought with her. "Most of the girls are there waiting for you."

"Thanks." She pulled her collar up against the cold, hastening her steps. "Hopefully we can wrap it up before noon. At least that's my goal."

"Well, I'm here all day," he said. "So take as long as you need. I doubt the girls will mind." He grinned. "They seem to have fallen in love with you."

She laughed. "Well, I'm pretty crazy about them too." As he walked her to the auditorium, she told him a little about some of the girls and how they'd responded positively to their fashion show makeovers. "I'm so glad that I did them one at a time. That gave us the chance to get acquainted. And some of them really opened up."

"That's great." He opened the door for her.

"Yeah, it's really been fun." She smiled, taking her bag from him. "Thanks for encouraging me to do it."

"Thank you!" He tipped his head as several girls came rushing up to meet her. "Your fans await."

She laughed as she went inside, greeting the girls. "Did the clothes make it here okay?" she asked as they walked up to the stage.

"Yeah, Savannah and a guy just brought the racks in."

Belinda set her bag in one of the auditorium chairs, extracting her CD player and clipboard and a few other things. "Okay, let's get this party started."

As the last few stragglers arrived, Belinda began to organize the girls, explaining the order they would go in and that they'd have help changing outfits backstage. Then, talking a little about posture and poise and attitude, she gave them lessons on how to walk a runway.

"Have you done this before?" Kelsey asked with interest.

Belinda made an embarrassed smile. "Yeah, I did some runway modeling during beauty school. Helped to cover my tuition."

The girls seemed impressed, which she decided was probably good since she really got their attention. She turned on the music and cranked it up, and the runway walking lessons began. Some girls really got it, attacking the runway with swagger and style, but others needed coaxing and encouragement. After about an hour, she felt like they'd made enough progress to move on to the dressing part of the dress rehearsal.

With only Savannah there to help her, it was a bit of a challenge, but she reminded the girls that her friends would be assisting behind the scenes on Saturday. After a rough first run-through, Belinda insisted they had to try again, and to her relief—although there were some good-natured complaints—no one really seemed to mind.

"I'm going to clock us this time," she told them. "Hopefully we can keep it under ninety minutes."

As the girls changed and strutted and changed again, Belinda tried to watch the process with objective eyes. And, honestly, she was worried. As hard as she'd tried to make this fashion show into a success, she felt uneasy. The girls were amateurs at best, and the outfits were, well, secondhand clothes. The whole thing, for all she knew, could fall totally flat.

As they were wrapping it up, she tried not to focus on all that was wrong—which seemed to be plenty. Instead, she would have to hope for the best and pray that the girls had an enjoyable time and that the attendees of the fashion show would not be disappointed. From what she could tell, ticket sales had been strong. She wasn't sure why or how that had happened, but she was impressed—and terrified.

"I want to go through one last runway strut," she told the girls after they were back in their own clothes. "Just so that you can have it fixed in your minds. And I want everyone to promise me to practice your strut at home. I want you all to be in fine strutting shape by Saturday. Okay?"

They all agreed, and she turned on the music again. Like before, she started them out, strutting her stuff like she was a supermodel at New York Fashion Week. The girls all clapped and then, one by one, imitated her. Finally, as if to reward them for their efforts, she did one final strut, laughing to herself as she realized that, at forty-five, she was a bit long in the tooth for modeling. Still it was fun. As she made her final turn at the end of her run, she heard the sound of enthusiastic clapping down in the auditorium.

"Mr. Trellis," someone called out. "Have you been watching us this whole time?"

He laughed. "No, I just stepped in."

Feeling embarrassed, Belinda turned off the music.

"Sorry to interrupt," he called out.

"It's okay," she called back. "We're finishing up." She went down the stairs to join him, speaking loudly so that the girls could hear. "The models are fabulous. I think they're ready for Saturday."

"That's great." He lowered his voice. "I actually stopped by to see if you had time to go to coffee with me—I mean, if you're done here. I don't want to rush you."

Was he asking her out? Her usual reaction to male attention like that was to make up an excuse. She'd been doing it for years. But seeing the hopeful expression in his eyes, and realizing that perhaps he wanted to discuss the girls and the fashion show, she accepted. "Let me have a last word with the girls and get my stuff," she said quietly, "and I'll meet you out by the administration office, okay?"

He nodded. "See you then."

Belinda gave the girls one last pep talk, then talked to Savannah about getting the clothes back to the shop and finally headed out to meet Carey. As she walked across the campus she felt a mixture of anticipation and nerves. Even if this wasn't a date per se, she knew that a part of her wanted it to be. And yet another part of her wanted to stick with her status quo. She was comfortable as a single woman. She was strong and independent and liked doing what she wanted to do when she wanted to do it. At least that was what she usually told herself—and anyone else who wanted to know. But the truth was she was lonely too. Especially since Emma went off to college three years ago.

Suddenly Belinda remembered her angel verse from Abby. God had good plans for her, plans for hope and a good future. What if those plans involved a man? Shouldn't she be open to that? Still, she was reluctant to get her hopes up. Especially with someone like Carey Trellis. If he let her down, the fall would be painful.

As she neared the admin offices, she prayed a silent prayer. If

Carey Trellis was truly part of God's good plans for her, God would have to make it happen. She sure couldn't. But knowing that helped her to relax some as Carey came out to meet her.

"I thought we could walk over to Starbucks," he said as he joined her. "That is, if you're warm enough." He checked her out more closely. "And if those stylish boots are good for walking."

She laughed. "Walking sounds lovely."

As they walked, he expressed even more gratitude for her work with the girls. "Some of the staff gave me a bad time for caring about something as seemingly insignificant as the way some of these girls dress. They said I was opening a can of worms to do this. But I kept thinking that if they were my daughters, I'd want someone to help them."

"I know." She nodded as they waited to cross the street. "I actually started Glad Rags because I was so unhappy with the way my daughter, Emma, and her friends were dressing when they were in middle school. Their excuse was that it was too expensive to dress stylishly—whatever that was back then. So I decided to show them how they could use redesigned resale clothes to have a really unique look."

"How old is your daughter?" he asked.

"Twenty. She's in her junior year at college."

He turned to look curiously at her. "You don't look old enough."

"Thanks. I was only twelve when I had her." She laughed. "Joking. I was actually in my early twenties." She suddenly regretted this. Why was she telling him her age? "What about you? Any kids?"

"We wanted to, but I insisted on waiting until we were both done with college and settled into good jobs. After that, Marley's illness made it impossible." He paused in front of Starbucks to open the door for her. "Sometimes I think that was a mistake."

"That old 20/20 hindsight," she said as they went inside.

Before long they were seated at a table and, as they sipped their coffees, they both began to open up, telling their stories and how they had reached the place in life where they were. Belinda didn't go into all the details of her failed marriage. "Suffice it to say that my ex didn't want to be married with children. He went his way and I stayed here. I don't really have regrets. I used to. But then I realized that my rotten marriage gave me Emma. She's worth it all." Belinda told him a bit more about Emma and all her accomplishments, and how proud she was of her girl.

He smiled. "She sounds like a lovely person."

Belinda's smile faded. "I'm just sad that she's not coming home for Christmas."

"Why not?"

"The boyfriend." Belinda grimaced. "And I really can't complain. Archer is a really great guy and I wouldn't be surprised if they get married. She's going home with him—to Connecticut—to meet Archer's family."

"So you're alone at Christmas?"

She sighed. "I would've gone to Abby and Clayton's, but Abby passed on." She looked down at her coffee, wondering why she was divulging so much.

"I'm alone at Christmas too," he said glumly. "My family is all in Southern California, and after this move and buying a house, it's not in the budget to go down there this year."

"I have some single friends," she said suddenly—without really thinking it through, although Cassidy and Louisa did come to mind. "I was considering inviting them to my place for Christmas. Maybe you could join us."

He brightened. "That'd be great. Thanks, I'd like that."

Now she'd gone and done it—Carey Trellis was coming to her house for Christmas. Hopefully he hadn't agreed out of plain old pity. And hopefully Louisa and Cassidy hadn't made plans yet. Belinda had less than a week to figure it all out. Or cancel. She could always cancel.

13

On Wednesday afternoon, Grace knew it was only a matter of time before her house would become busy and noisy again—the twins would be home from college tomorrow evening and, knowing them, a bunch of their friends would be hanging out there too. And although Grace had apologized to Joel for several things, she still hadn't had a good opportunity to tell him about what was going on inside her. She wanted the chance to do that before her house turned into Grand Central Station.

That was why she called Joel from work, making sure that he would be home by a decent hour and informing him that she would be fixing dinner. "Just for the two of us," she said in a mysterious tone.

"That sounds interesting." But she could hear the question mark in his voice—as if he suspected she might have ulterior motives. As she put her phone away, she had to ask herself . . . Had she really been that manipulative? Was that how Joel perceived her?

As she drove home from the grocery store, she saw a few

snowflakes flying. Were they really going to have a white Christmas like the weatherman had been predicting? Perhaps she should've stocked up more provisions. And what about the twins driving home tomorrow—what if they got stuck in a blizzard?

She pulled into her driveway, reminding herself of Matthew 6 and what it said about worrying. She needed to trust God for provision and protection—and stop fretting. She continued to remind herself of these things as she fixed a simple dinner for Joel and her. As tempting as it was to start obsessing over all the various details and demands of her life, she was determined to trust God. Otherwise, she felt certain she would completely lose it.

When Joel came home she greeted him with a hug and a kiss. "Did you see snow on your way home?" she asked.

He looked at her with a puzzled expression, like he was thinking, *Who are you, and what have you done with my wife?* Fortunately, he didn't say this. "Yeah, some flakes were flying around out there. Hopefully it'll hold out until the kids get home."

"I'm sure they'll be fine. Even if it does snow, it will be an adventure, right?"

He blinked as he removed his coat.

"Dinner's almost ready," she said as she went to check on the wild rice. "Just fish and veggies and rice. But I know you don't like heavy dinners."

"Sounds good." He followed her into the kitchen. "You okay, Grace?"

She turned to smile at him. "Sure. Why wouldn't I be?"

"It's just that you're acting weird." He narrowed his eyes slightly. "Like you're about to say something like, 'We need to talk.'"

"Well, we *do* need to talk."

He looked truly alarmed.

"Not like that," she assured him. "I'm not about to run off and have an affair or anything stupid like that."

"Oh . . . good." He still looked perplexed as he pulled out a counter stool to sit before a small plate of appetizers she'd set out. "What's up then?"

"There are some things I want to share with you," she said mysteriously.

His brow creased with concern. "You're not sick, are you? You're not about to tell me you've got cancer or something?"

She patted his hand. "No, nothing like that. Don't be such a worrier."

He smiled. "Oh, that's right. That's your job. You're the little worrywart."

"Not anymore."

He frowned. "What do you mean?"

"I mean I'm trying to change some things." Then, as they sat down to eat, she explained about Matthew 6 and her new outlook. She told him about the Habitat project and how she was trying to fly beneath the radar on it. "I don't want anyone to know I'm responsible for it."

"Because it's so bad?" he questioned.

"No, it's actually turning out really great. Miraculously great. But I want to give God the credit. That's part of that Bible chapter. But it's more than just that." She told him about the money part. "I know that we used to say that we trusted God to provide for us. Back when we were newly married and broke. But somehow we kind of lost track of that. It's like we started to believe we were in charge of everything. And we started to worry and fight and, well, it got very stressful."

Joel nodded as he chewed. "I can't disagree about the stressful part, but I'm not really sure how to do what you're saying. We still have bills to pay, Grace. It's not like we can just throw in the towel and give up. Expect God to drop down pennies from heaven."

"I know. But I think I've come to realize that having my own design firm downtown might've been a bad idea."

His eyes lit up. "Really?"

"I know, you always thought that from the start." She tried to suppress her urge to defend herself.

"Not exactly. I mean, I always wanted you to do what made you happy, Grace. I knew you were a great designer. But the timing of it . . . well, you know. With the twins about to head to college and the real estate market still slumping, I questioned it."

"I know. And you were probably right."

He stared at her with a bewildered look.

"The reality is that I've been more stressed than ever since I opened the design studio. Lately I've been wishing that I was still working from home. You know?"

"Well, you can always do that. I mean, if you want to, Grace. I won't tell you what to do. I know how well that works." He grinned.

They continued to talk—about their jobs, their lives, their kids, and money . . . and for the first time in ages, it felt like they were really connecting. Like it was old times.

"I sort of wish the twins weren't coming home tomorrow," he said as they were cleaning up the dinner dishes together. "I wouldn't mind it just being me and you for a few more days."

She laughed. "Well, they'll be so busy with their friends, I wouldn't be too concerned. And before you know it, they'll be gone again anyway. We should enjoy them while they're here." She held up a finger. "And if you don't mind, I would appreciate it if you didn't harp on them about their grades too much. If you need to say something, why not get it over with as soon as they get here and then we can move on. I don't want our time together to turn out like Thanksgiving. Okay?"

He nodded as he slipped his arms around her waist, pulling her to him. "Yeah. You're right."

"I've missed you," she said quietly.

"Me too." He bent down to kiss her. "It's been too long."

Louisa felt inexplicably happy as she puttered around her house on Thursday afternoon. She knew that her lifted spirits were directly related to her art therapy class. She'd led the second one that morning and, to her delight, everyone from last week had showed up again. Their projects today had gone well—and the sharing was even better than the previous Thursday. The only downside was that they wouldn't meet again for two weeks. But that was simply because of Christmas.

As she got her house ready for tonight's angels' meeting, with Christmas music playing on her ancient stereo, she felt that old spring in her step again. She paused to look at the Bible verse that she'd found tucked inside her angel ornament. She'd taped it to the refrigerator so that she could look at it frequently. It was Isaiah 40:31, and the promise was that those who hoped and waited on the Lord would fly like eagles—they would run without tiring and walk without getting weary.

Because she'd been so tired and weary—after losing Adam and then Abby—Louisa had really grabbed onto that verse. And every morning for nearly a week, she'd taken the time to sit quietly in her living room with a cup of tea and her Bible, waiting on the Lord. Already, she felt stronger. Even after her art therapy class today, she was still energized. She couldn't wait to see the angels and to hear how their week had gone.

The first to arrive was Grace, and she looked a little worn out. "Come get yourself something to eat and drink," Louisa told her as she led Grace to the dining room. "You look like you need it."

"Thank you." Grace sighed. "It's been a long week."

"So how is your Habitat project going?"

Grace smiled brightly. "Thanks to everyone's help and contributions, it's coming together beautifully. Everything is falling right into place—almost on its own." She laughed. "As if it would come together even if I wasn't involved."

"Interesting." Louisa studied her closely.

"And your paintings," Grace told her. "I cannot even tell you what a difference they've made in the rooms. I hope you go to the open house on Sunday to see how good they look. It's nothing short of miraculous." She sighed as she stirred cream into her decaf. "I really have to give God the credit. I never could've pulled this off on my own."

Louisa blinked in surprise. This didn't sound like Grace. But it sounded good. "That's wonderful," she told her. "I'm sure the new homeowners will feel very blessed by your efforts."

"Not my efforts," Grace said quickly. "It's thanks to all the lovely donations from generous folks like you, Louisa." She told her how good some of Louisa's old furnishings had looked in the rooms. "It's the sort of thing a designer can't plan," she explained. "All the pieces came from different places and for all intents and purposes should never have worked—and yet they do. It's truly a God thing."

Cassidy and Belinda were coming in now and, although Louisa was curious to hear more about Grace's project, she went to greet them. Louisa invited them to get food and drinks and then, as they settled in the living room, she asked Grace to continue telling them about her project.

"Grace is giving God all the credit for the Habitat homes

coming together so nicely," Louisa told the others. "It sounds as if it's a miracle."

"A miracle that had very little to do with me," Grace explained. "I never could've pulled it off on my own." She smiled at them. "And, besides God, I have all of you to thank. Your contributions were absolutely perfect. I hope everyone will attend the open house on Sunday." She pointed to Belinda. "And now I want to hear how your fashion show is coming. Do you still need us on Saturday?"

"Absolutely." Belinda told them about her dress rehearsal and how hard the girls were working. "But I'm worried," she confessed. "The whole thing could so easily fall apart. It's not that I care so much for my own sake, but I really don't want to see the girls embarrassed or hurt by this. I want it to be a success so they'll feel good about it and good about themselves. That's really what it's all about."

"We'll do everything we can to help ensure this," Louisa told her.

They discussed the ins and outs of Saturday's fashion show for a few minutes. Finally Louisa looked at Cassidy. "You're being awfully quiet tonight. What's going on with you?"

Cassidy looked close to tears. "Nothing much."

"What is it, Cass?" Belinda asked with compassionate eyes. "Tell us."

"It's just that—well, it feels like everything is going wrong. Dr. Auberon wants to pull the plug on my volunteer work. He says people are getting confused, thinking that it's a service that he's offering. He's worried pet owners are going to complain about paying for appointments. I tried to explain that it's not like that. I tell anyone I help that it's not related to Auberon Animal Hospital. But he won't listen. He said I have to stop or he'll let me go."

"Oh, Cassidy." Louisa shook her head. "That's not right."

"I know." Cassidy's chin quivered. "I already bought a bunch of vaccines and meds. What am I supposed to do with them? And I have pet owners who are counting on me. But I can't afford to keep doing the volunteer stuff without a way to support myself. It's such a mess."

"Have you prayed about it?" Grace asked.

Cassidy blinked at her. "Well, yeah, of course."

"I know," Grace said almost apologetically. "You guys don't think of me as the praying type. But I'm changing. This angel project has helped me to see things differently."

"That's great," Louisa told her. She wanted to add that she could see that Grace was different, but didn't want to offend her.

"So how did your date with the grandson go?" Belinda asked Cassidy. "What was he like?"

"Brent Morgan was . . . he was . . . *fabulous*!" Now Cassidy broke down into full-blown tears.

Louisa moved over to sit on the sofa next to Cassidy, wrapping an arm around her shoulders. "If he was fabulous, why are you crying?"

"Because he didn't like me," she sobbed.

"How do you know that?" Belinda demanded. "I mean, if he was fabulous. What did he do?"

"He couldn't wait to get away from me—he couldn't leave fast enough."

"Oh, well." Belinda bit her lip. "Then he's not worth fretting over."

"Yes." Louisa nodded firmly. "You're better off without him."

"But Brent was fabulous!" Cassidy insisted.

"If he was that fabulous, he would've seen how fabulous you are," Grace argued.

They all commiserated with Cassidy for a bit, and finally,

she blew her nose and sat up straighter. "I'm sorry to be such a baby."

"You're not a baby," Louisa assured her. "You just got hurt, that's all. We understand."

"I think I need to give up on men altogether." Cassidy nodded firmly. "I can be happy and be single." She pointed to Belinda. "Just like you've been all these years, Belinda. You're an inspiration. Seriously, if you can do it, so can I."

Belinda gave them a slightly sheepish expression, as if this was somehow not quite true—and then she actually giggled.

"What's up with you?" Grace asked her. "What are you keeping from us?"

"Is there a man in your life?" Louisa demanded.

"Not exactly." Belinda sighed. "But somehow I managed to invite the principal of McKinley High to join me for Christmas."

"What?" Louisa stared at Belinda. For all the years she'd known her, she couldn't recall one time when Belinda had brought a fellow home for the holidays. What was going on?

"It's only that he's single and he was going to be alone for Christmas," she said quickly. "So I mentioned I have some single friends." She clasped her hands together. "Please, I'm begging you guys. Say you'll come to my house for Christmas—*please!*"

"I'd be glad to," Louisa told her.

"I don't have anyone to spend Christmas with," Cassidy muttered. "Why would I?"

"I know you probably have plans with your kids and family," Belinda told Grace. "But you'd all be welcome too."

Grace nodded. "Let me get back to you on that."

They continued to chat and plan, and next thing they knew it was getting late. But before Louisa would let them leave, she insisted on a prayer. "I think if Abby were here, she would agree," Louisa said somewhat apologetically. "I'd like to pray for Belinda's girls and the fashion show on Saturday. And for Grace's open house on Sunday." She turned to where Cassidy was still sitting with a dejected expression. "And for Cassidy's future as well as her hurting heart." Then Louisa led them in a prayer. And it felt good.

14

Belinda would've liked to say that the fashion show went off without a glitch, but that wasn't quite true. It was, however, a triumph. At least as far as she was concerned. Sure, some girls missed their cues. One girl tripped on the steps. And there were a couple of wardrobe malfunctions—nothing serious, just awkward.

Belinda knew she never could've pulled it off without the help of her angel friends. While she emceed the show, Louisa managed the roster and kept everything moving along fairly smoothly. Grace supervised hair and makeup, mostly to assure the girls didn't apply more makeup than needed. Especially since Belinda had gotten them essentially ready before the show. Cassidy helped Savannah with wardrobe and changing.

Belinda thanked her dear friends afterward with luxurious gift bags she'd prepared earlier in the week. "I owe you all big-time," she said as she hugged each of them goodbye. "I'll see you tomorrow afternoon at the open house." She winked at Grace. "It'll be your turn to shine."

Grace solemnly shook her head. "I don't want to shine." She smiled. "But I do want the homes to sparkle."

After her friends left, Belinda gathered with her models in the dressing area. As she thanked and congratulated the girls, she was surprised by the tears and the hugs and gratitude. "You all did a fantastic job," she told them. "You were really amazing. And did you see how many people came?" She took a moment to present the gift certificate prize to the girl who'd sold the most tickets. "I'm so impressed, Amelia," she told the quiet girl. "You might have a future in sales." She smiled at the rest of them. "And I hope you all enjoy your outfits. You all look beautiful." She had planned the show so that they modeled their gifted outfits last. That way they could wear them home.

"This was the best day of my life," Remmie said as she hugged Belinda again. "Thank you so much!"

The others gushed their appreciation as well. So much so that Belinda was starting to feel self-conscious. "Remember, you girls are the ones who did the hard work," she said. "I simply organized it." She reached for her bag and coat. "And don't forget my offer." Belinda reminded them of the idea that she and Carey had come up with over coffee the other day. "You're all invited to intern at Glad Rags. Mr. Trellis will make the arrangements with Mrs. Wilcox in the business department in January. So really think about it, okay?"

They all seemed eager to intern, and Belinda was already imagining ways she'd keep them busy. But the truth was she'd be surprised if they all signed up. "You girls gather up your stuff from home. Try not to leave anything behind." She exchanged a glance with Savannah. "I've got to get back to the shop. You all have a very Merry Christmas!"

They echoed her greeting, calling out more goodbyes and

"I love yous" as she hurried out the back door. There, to her surprise, she ran smack into Carey Trellis.

"Oh!" She caught her balance and he steadied her with one hand.

"I was hoping to run into you." He chuckled. "Well, not literally, but hey, it works."

"I was telling the girls goodbye." She paused to button up her coat.

"I bet they didn't want to let you go."

She smiled. "They make me feel kind of like a rock star."

"In their eyes you are a rock star." He walked with her toward her car. "I was wondering if you're busy . . ."

"Right now?" She glanced at her watch. "I really need to get to my shop. I promised Mimi that I'd relieve her by four."

"What about later?" he persisted. "Any chance I can entice you to have dinner with me?"

She tilted her head to one side. "Are you asking me on a date, Mr. Trellis?"

He grinned nervously. "I am, *Ms. Michaels*. But I thought we were already on a first-name basis."

"Okay then, yes, I'd like to have dinner with you, Carey."

"Is seven okay?"

"I'll make it okay," she told him, knowing she'd have to talk Savannah into closing for her tonight. But if Savannah knew it was for a date, she'd probably be more than willing. Savannah had been nagging Belinda to go out for ages.

Carey offered to pick her up, and she told him where she lived. It wasn't until she was driving back to her shop that it really hit her. She was going on a date with Carey Trellis. A warm rush of anticipation surged through her—*she was going on a date!* A real date! And she actually wanted to go. She wondered what Emma would think when she told her. Of course, she'd probably be happy for her, but she'd probably be a little uneasy too. Sometimes it felt like Emma assumed that Belinda would always be the same—her hardworking single mom. To be fair, it was probably Belinda's fault, since that was how she always portrayed herself. A no-nonsense, independent, set-in-her-ways, single woman.

"It's not like he's proposed marriage to you," she said to herself as she parked behind her shop. "He asked you to dinner, silly. And it's probably just his way to thank you for working with 'his' girls." Yes, she decided as she went inside. That was it. Carey simply wanted to show his appreciation for the fashion show. And why not? Belinda had invested a lot of time and energy into it. She'd done it more for the girls than for him. Still, it would be nice to be appreciated.

It was after five by the time Savannah got back. As Belinda helped her unload the clothes into the back room, she told her about her dinner plans.

"You're going out with Carey Trellis?" Savannah cried.

"We're merely having dinner together." Belinda picked up a blouse from the floor. "I'm sure he only wants to thank me for—"

"You're not *that* dense." Savannah waved a finger at her. "Haven't you seen how that man gapes at you? And, by the way, have you noticed how good-looking he is? Good grief, Belinda, the first time I saw him I thought he was Denzel Washington— you know, back in Denzel's younger days. You're going on a date, Belinda Michaels, and I suggest you get yourself home and get ready for it. I'll take care of everything here."

With a little more prodding, Belinda finally gave in. As busy as she'd been with the fashion show, the girls, and running her shop, she knew her own beauty routine had been slipping. Maybe it was time to spend some energy on her own image for a change.

By seven, Belinda felt like a new woman. She'd enjoyed a nice soak in the tub, given herself a manicure, done her hair, and finally dressed in what she hoped was an appropriate outfit—since she hadn't asked where they were going. But her plum-colored knit dress with her tall brown boots would fit most restaurants. If Carey planned to take her bowling, they might have problems. In her usual style, she layered on some jewelry—dangly earrings, a couple of interesting cuffs, and a long, simple necklace. If she was doling out fashion advice, she usually warned women that less was more when it came to jewelry accessories. But since her outfit was simple and she was tall, she thought it worked. According to her full-length mirror it worked.

And, even though she still kept telling herself that this date might only be a thank-you date, she suspected that it was something more. She hoped it was something more. When her doorbell rang, she reminded herself of the verse that had been hidden in her angel. God had good plans for her . . . a good future.

"You look stunning," Carey told her as she invited him in.

"So do you." She nodded approval at his stylish sports jacket, gray shirt, and dark tie, relieved that he wasn't wearing a bowling shirt.

"I like your house." He glanced around. "Very homey."

"It was actually my mother's house. She left it to me. Sometimes I think I should sell it and move on—you know, into something that's more modern and hip, more my style. But then I remember all the good times we had here, the memories . . . and I can't imagine letting it go. Besides that, Emma would kill me. I'm supposed to leave it to her." She laughed. "Not that I'm going anywhere anytime soon."

"Besides to dinner." He checked his watch. "Our reservation is for 7:15, so we should probably go."

Belinda felt almost like she was in a dream as he walked her to his car, opened the door, and helped her in. She'd never been on a date where a guy had been that gentlemanly—and, she decided, she liked it!

"I know, I know," he said as he started the car. "I'm old-fashioned about manners. Some women have even called me chauvinistic because I want to open doors for them. But it's how I was brought up."

"Your mama raised you right." She laughed. "My mama would approve."

"I got us in at the Tree House."

"Are you kidding?" She turned to stare at him. "I've been dying to go there, but I heard that their waiting list was months out. How did you manage that?"

He chuckled. "It's the old case of not *what* you know, but *who* you know. It's owned by the parents of one of my students at McKinley."

"So you used your principal clout?"

"I only mentioned the student's name and that I was the principal and new in town, and voila—it worked like magic."

Everything about the evening felt magical—or maybe *miraculous* was the right word. As they were driving home, Belinda decided she'd have to give the three Cs an A+. The company, the conversation, and the cuisine had all been superb. It was so enjoyable that she really didn't want the evening to end.

But she started to feel nervous when Carey walked her to her house. Hopefully he didn't expect her to invite him in. "I had a lovely time," she told him. "Everything was perfect."

"Thank you for going with me," he said as he lingered on her porch.

"Thank you for taking me." She felt a fluttering inside her as she gazed into his dark eyes. "I'd invite you in, Carey, but

I—uh—the truth is, I'm really not comfortable with that. I suppose it's from having raised my daughter, you know, trying to set a good example."

He smiled. "I was hoping you were an old-fashioned girl, Belinda."

Relief washed over her and she knew this was the kind of guy that was worth waiting for—even if she had waited for more than twenty years.

"Would it be okay if I kissed you good night?" he asked.

Feeling like a teenager again, she simply nodded. And just like that, he leaned toward her and she felt herself being swept away in his kiss. The perfect kiss.

"Oh. . ." She sighed, trying to maintain her balance.

"I know you invited me here for Christmas," he said as he stepped back, "but that's several days away. Do you mind if I call before then?"

She felt her heart soaring. "Not at all."

His face lit up in a smile. "Good night then, Belinda. I'll be in touch."

As she turned to go inside, she felt like she was floating. Literally floating. Was this really for real? And then she remembered that verse again—God had *good* plans for her, plans for a *good* future. She believed it!

Grace was tempted to wear a disguise to the Habitat open house on Sunday. Not that she thought she was some recognizable celebrity, but she didn't want any of the attention to land on her. She'd been successfully maintaining a low profile lately and had declined the invitation to place her design placard in the rooms she'd assembled.

"I don't think it's necessary," she'd told the director of the project several days ago. "It would take away from the overall design." Fortunately, he didn't dispute this, so the living rooms in all three houses were without placards. And really, she decided, who cared?

She stood at the back of the crowd at the first ribbon-cutting ceremony, clapping supportively as several speeches were made, but happy to remain behind the scenes. Joel, who'd been informed of her need for anonymity, didn't seem to mind as he stood beside her, holding her hand. They sipped their coffees as they stood outside, waiting as the homeowners went inside to look around. Before long, the others began to go in to tour the home and, finally, after the crowd had thinned, Grace and Joel walked through.

"You did a great job," Joel whispered to her. "It looks really warm and inviting."

She simply smiled, glad that no one was nearby to overhear him. As they toured the small house, she told him a little about the family who'd be living there and how long they'd been waiting to own a home. "It's so wonderful how Habitat works. Such a community project."

"And impressive they could simultaneously put up three homes—and all completely furnished."

"It does make you feel good, doesn't it?" She let out a happy sigh. "To be part of such a generous community."

The next two houses' ceremonies were similar. Although Grace's angel friends were there, they all remembered her request not to mention that she'd had any involvement in the projects. She even kept her interaction with the homeowners brief and low-key—mostly just congratulating them on their new homes and wishing them a Merry Christmas!

When all was said and done, she was relieved to go home. "I'm so glad that's over with," she told Joel as they pulled up to their own house, which she'd finally managed to decorate for Christmas. She'd given herself permission to hold back some, so the décor was not as excessive as usual, but it was enough.

"Looks like the kids are home," Joel said as he pulled into the driveway.

"And their friends too," she added, "judging by the cars out front."

"I bet we could sneak away for a quiet little early dinner—just the two of us—and no one would even miss us."

"Do you want to?" she asked hopefully.

"Let's do it!" He sounded eager. "Let's run away from home for a couple hours."

Feeling like renegades, they hightailed it out of there. At the café, as they sat together talking about the day and what was ahead for the holidays, Grace felt like she'd been given a second chance—not only in her marriage but in life as well.

15

It was the Monday before Christmas, and Cassidy felt like a failure. She knew that was an overstatement, but it seemed like nothing was going quite right. Her job at Auberon Animal Hospital had been put at risk by her volunteer work. Her volunteer work was about to be extinguished by her job at the vet clinic. And her personal life . . . well, she didn't even want to go there.

"You are *not* a failure," Belinda said for the third time as the two of them met at the Coffee Cup after Cassidy got off work. "You're in a tough spot—between a rock and a hard place."

"Dr. Auberon gave me until after Christmas to make up my mind."

"What're you going to do?"

Cassidy let out a long sigh. "I need to make a living."

Belinda simply nodded.

"But it makes me so sad to give up that dream." Cassidy sighed again.

"Maybe it's a timing thing," Belinda suggested. "Something you need to work toward. When I was doing hair, I knew that I wanted to do some kind of resale shop, but I had to keep doing hair for a while . . . until the timing was right and I was ready to open a shop. And even then, I could only afford to open a tiny shop, and all I carried was baby and kid stuff. It took a lot of time and work to grow it up to Glad Rags."

Cassidy nodded. "Yeah, that makes sense."

"I think if it's meant to be—if you're supposed to have a mobile pet care business, which I think is a wonderful idea—it will happen. But it might take some time."

"And in the meantime, I should keep my day job." Cassidy attempted a feeble smile.

"Maybe so."

"That's kind of what I've been thinking too. It's hard letting the dream go."

"Sometimes we have to let our dreams go in order to allow God to bring them back to us—in his way and his timing." Belinda grinned. "That's what my mama used to tell me. Honestly, I never liked hearing those words. I wanted to run ahead and make my dreams come true all by myself. But the older I get, the more I understand it."

"Okay." Cassidy set down her empty mug with fresh resolve. "That's what I'm going to do."

"Good for you." Belinda pointed to Cassidy's bag, which was ringing. "Is that your phone?"

Cassidy fished out her phone to see she had a text. "It's from Brent Morgan."

"Brent Morgan?"

"Dorothy Morgan's grandson—the fabulous guy who didn't like me."

"Why's he texting you?"

"I have no idea. He wants me to meet him at his grandma's place this afternoon."

"Are you going?"

Cassidy felt unsure. "I don't know."

"This is the first time you've heard from him since that dinner?"

Cassidy nodded, staring down at the phone. "I didn't even know he had my number. I guess he got it from Dorothy."

"What does he do anyway? I don't recall if you mentioned it."

"I think Dorothy said that he's a computer engineer. He works from home, then travels to do consulting." Cassidy set down her phone.

"Aren't you curious?" Belinda's eyes lit up. "Maybe he wants to apologize to you, Cass. Maybe he realized that he blew it and wants to make it up."

Cassidy shook her head. "I doubt it."

"So you're going to just ignore him?"

"No . . ." Cassidy suddenly texted him back, agreeing to meet. "I want to hear what he's got to say."

"Good for you."

Cassidy waited to see if he was responding. "Sounds like he's there right now. He wants me to stop by."

"What're you waiting for?"

They stood and said goodbye, and soon Cassidy found herself nervously driving through the wind-driven snow across town. Why did Brent want her to come to his grandmother's apartment? Was something wrong with Dorothy? Or Muffin perhaps? As she parked at the apartments, Cassidy wished she had on something more attractive than her scrubs. But at least she could let her hair out of the ponytail and smear on some lip gloss. And then she wondered, as she knocked on the door, why had she bothered?

"There you are!" Brent smiled wide as he opened the door, waving her inside. "Come on in out of that blizzard!" He peered over her shoulder. "Man, it's really coming down now."

"Welcome," Dorothy called out. "I've got hot water for tea."

Cassidy went inside, trying to act natural as she greeted both of them and pretending that Brent's abrupt departure hadn't hurt her feelings the other night. "I like your little Christmas tree," she told Dorothy lightly as she shook the snow off her parka. "Very festive."

"Brent brought that. He just got back from New York. Missed the bad weather too." Dorothy led Cassidy toward the kitchen. "He stopped by here, even before going home. He said he noticed the tree lot near the airport. Sweet boy! And he's been helping me to decorate it too."

"How nice." Cassidy wished she knew what was going on as she sat down at the dinette where a plate of homemade Christmas cookies and three teacups were all set up. "Looks like a Christmas tea party," she said absently, trying not to feel like Alice being hosted by the Mad Hatter. *What is going on?*

"Brent has good news for you," Dorothy said as she set a teapot on the table.

"Good news?" Cassidy studied Brent as he sat down across from her.

"Well, first I should apologize for running ahead," he began. "Grandma can tell you that I've always been impetuous and impulsive."

"Oh, my, yes." Dorothy started telling a story about when a ten-year-old Brent decided to have a garage sale. "Without consulting his parents." She shook her head. "Before they knew what had happened, Brent had made about fifty dollars selling things out of their garage."

"My mom had been complaining about how crowded our garage was, saying how we needed to get rid of stuff," Brent explained innocently.

"But selling your dad's new golf clubs for ten dollars?" Dorothy chuckled.

"Mom made me go buy them back from the neighbor," Brent told Cassidy. "Fortunately, he didn't up the price."

Despite her general discomfort over this mysterious tea party, Cassidy laughed.

"Anyway, when I heard your idea about being a mobile vet—and I could see how passionate you were about it—I got an idea."

"A wonderful idea," Dorothy said eagerly.

"It hit me at dinner and it took all my self-control to keep it to myself," Brent told Cassidy.

"That's why Brent left so quickly that night," Dorothy explained. "He wanted to go speak to his uncle Rob—that's his mother's brother." She arched her brows. "Very wealthy man."

"After I left, I felt bad for running off so quickly," Brent explained. "But I knew I was leaving for New York the next morning and I thought if I could talk to Uncle Rob before I left, well, it seemed worth the effort."

"You see, Rob is an animal advocate," Dorothy told Cassidy.

"That's right," Brent continued. "My uncle supports a number of worthwhile animal causes, and it hit me that a mobile veterinarian business might be the sort of thing he'd be interested in. And I was so enthused over this idea—plus I knew I wouldn't be back until right before Christmas—that I decided to run over to his house and talk to him about it."

The wheels in Cassidy's head were starting to turn now. "So you didn't eat and run because you couldn't stand me?" *Whoops! Why did I say that? How pathetic!*

Brent laughed. "Are you kidding me?"

She shrugged. "Well, it felt sort of like that."

"I'm so sorry, Cassidy." He looked genuinely apologetic. "I

didn't think about how you might feel. I just didn't want to miss an opportunity with my uncle. Especially since I knew that he was taking his family to Aspen for the holidays. They won't be back until after New Year's. I felt like there was no time to waste."

Cassidy nodded, but it felt like her head was spinning ever so slightly.

"Well, tell her how it went," Dorothy said eagerly. "Tell her what Rob said, Brent."

"Uncle Rob is very interested in your idea. And he wants to meet you, Cassidy. I think he might like to partner with your mobile veterinarian business. He thinks you should consider making it a not-for-profit corporation—that way you make a living but get some tax breaks."

"Really?" She felt slightly dizzy. Brent didn't hate her and his uncle was interested in her crazy idea? Was she dreaming?

"Uncle Rob obviously needs to get to know you first, but based on what I told him, he was very, very interested. He asked me to bring you to meet him in early January."

Cassidy felt tears coming into her eyes. "*Seriously?*"

"Would you be open to partnering with a financial backer?" he asked. "I can assure you that Uncle Rob is a trustworthy guy. He even gave me a list of some of the animal foundations that he supports. They're all well respected. And so is he."

"Wow." She blinked, trying to contain her tears of joy. "That's so amazing. I don't even know what to say. Of course I'm interested! I can't wait to meet your uncle. It's like a dream come true!"

Dorothy held up her teacup. "I think this deserves a toast."

Brent lifted his cup too. "Here's to Cassidy's mobile vet business—may it take off in the coming year."

They sat around the little dinette table talking excitedly about the possibilities. She even confided to them about her boss's recent ultimatum. "I didn't want to give up volunteering," she admitted, "but I do need to support myself."

"Well, it sounds like you'll be able to do both now," Dorothy declared.

After the tea and cookies were gone, Cassidy thanked them and, not wanting to wear out her welcome, wished them a Merry Christmas.

"Wait," Brent said as he walked her to the door. "What are you doing for dinner tonight?"

"For dinner?" She peered curiously at him. Was he asking her out?

"Yeah. I know it's a little early, but I think I'm still on East Coast time. And I've been craving barbecue for the past few days."

"Barbecue?" She tipped her head to one side.

He helped her into her parka, then reached for his own coat. "There's a great place over on First Street. Those Christmas cookies were good, but I never had lunch. You hungry for an early dinner? Like barbecue?"

She smiled. "I love barbecue."

"What're we waiting for?" He kissed his grandma goodbye, and suddenly they were walking out into a winter wonderland. "Want to drop your car at your place before the snow gets too deep?" he suggested. "I can follow you and take you from there. That way you won't have to drive in the snow when it gets bad later. My Jeep can pretty much handle anything."

"Sounds like a good idea," she told him. "That way I can change out of my scrubs at my condo—if you're not too ravenous and don't mind waiting."

"No problem." He grinned at her. "I don't mind waiting. Not for you."

A warm rush ran through her as she hurried to her car and used her sleeve to wipe the windows clean. None of this seemed real. But, she decided, if this was a dream, she just wanted to keep it going. "Don't wake me up," she said as she started her car.

Louisa had invited her angel friends to gather at her house for a small, intimate brunch on Christmas Eve morning. Later that evening they would reconvene at Belinda's house with other guests, and then on Christmas Day they'd all been invited to a buffet dinner at Grace and Joel's. Lots of festivities and fun. Louisa hoped she could keep up.

"I'm so glad we could meet," Louisa told them as they sat together around her dining room table. "Thank you all for making the time to come here. I know you're all busy. But I hoped we could catch up. A chance for the Christmas Angels to share a final report."

"I'm so glad you asked us over," Cassidy said with enthusiasm. "I've been dying to tell you guys what's been going on with me, but I've been so busy these past several days, I just didn't have time." She grinned. "Besides, I wanted to tell you all at the same time."

"Tell us what?" Louisa asked her.

"Remember how devastated I was over Brent Morgan?" Cassidy explained that Brent had never meant to be rude, but that he'd simply wanted to help her by telling his investor uncle about her dream business. "And remember how I told you that Brent was fabulous? Well, I was right. He really is fabulous. We've spent the last few days together—when I'm not at work anyway. We've gone ice-skating and caroling with his church and to a Christmas play and all sorts of stuff. It's been truly amazing."

"Sounds like someone is falling in love," Grace teased.

Cassidy's cheeks were flushed and her eyes were bright as she giggled. "I think that's a possibility. But I'm trying to take it one day at a time. I don't want to scare him off, you know? I keep worrying he'll get tired of me, but he keeps calling." She pointed to Belinda. "In fact, I hope it's okay that I invited him to your house tonight."

"That's great," Belinda told her. "The more the merrier."

"And his grandmother too?" Cassidy asked hopefully.

"Absolutely. I can't wait to meet both of them."

"I guess that's about all the news I have," Cassidy said. "At least for now."

"Well, I've got some news," Belinda announced with brightly shining eyes. "But first I want to thank you girls. Because of our angels' project, this has turned into one of my best Christmases ever." She began telling them about her new relationship with the high school principal. "I doubt that I would've gotten to know Carey Trellis if Louisa hadn't challenged us to become Christmas angels this year." She beamed at Louisa. "Thank you for your inspiration. It was exactly what I needed."

"I need to thank all of you too," Louisa said. "You ladies really helped me to get out of my depressed slump this year. I never would've guessed that helping others deal with their own losses would make such a difference in my own life. But it has." She smiled gratefully at each of them. "Thank you all for encouraging me. In my book, you truly are earth angels."

"I guess it's my turn," Grace said after a brief pause. "I need to express some gratitude as well." She slowly shook her head. "I cannot even imagine where I'd be right now if you girls hadn't been in my life these past several weeks. To be honest, I was in a bad place. My kids weren't doing well. And my marriage was in trouble. I wasn't even sure Joel and I would get through it."

"Sometimes it takes a rough patch to get your attention," Louisa said.

Grace nodded. "I agree. But now we're doing better. Much better than we've done in years. I'm very grateful. And I'm grateful for our angel project. It's helped to change my perspective about a lot of things."

"Well, your living rooms in those Habitat homes certainly turned out nicely," Louisa told her.

"I couldn't have done any of that without your generous donations. Those poor families would probably be sitting on beanbag chairs and apple crates right now." Grace looked around the table. "I'm so thankful for all of you. I felt completely alone after Abby passed. But you girls have become true friends to me, and I hope that even if we don't have book group anymore and even if we're done with our Christmas angel project, we will continue being friends."

"Of course we will," Louisa assured her.

"But what about our book group?" Belinda asked. "Are we really done with that?"

"And our angel projects?" Cassidy questioned. "Was that only for Christmastime?"

"How does one retire from being an angel?" Louisa asked with a furrowed brow.

"I can't help thinking that Abby knew she was going to die," Cassidy said suddenly. "Somehow she had to have known. And that's why she made those ornaments and tucked in our secret Scripture verses. Because she knew she'd be gone and that we'd need each other more than ever."

"I've had the same thought," Belinda admitted.

"Abby would be very happy to see how the angel projects helped us to forge our friendships," Grace said quietly.

"It gives meaning to her death," Belinda said.

"I've been looking at death differently lately," Louisa confided. "Losing Adam and then Abby has changed my thinking. If you don't mind, I'd like to share something I recently said to my art therapy group." She paused to consider her words. "It's as if heaven has grown closer somehow. It used to feel so far away and otherworldly. But knowing that my loved ones are already there makes it seem more real. As if I now have a more direct connection. Does that make sense?"

They nodded as if they understood what she was trying to say.

"To be honest, I wanted to give up after Abby died," Louisa admitted. "I wanted to call it a day and go join her and Adam up there. But, after leading the art therapy classes and getting to know you ladies better, I don't feel like giving up anymore. In fact, I feel surprisingly energized. I want to make the most of every single day that I have left down here." She smiled. "Who knows how many days there are?"

"So what about continuing to meet?" Cassidy asked eagerly. "Can we keep being a book group or an angel group or something?"

"Why don't we do both? We can be an angel book group," Louisa suggested.

"An angel book group," Belinda echoed. "Interesting. I like it."

"And I know the book we should start with," Grace declared.

"What book?" Cassidy asked.

With a sly smile, Grace suggested they read the Bible. "Not the whole thing, of course. Maybe we should simply focus on one chapter, like Abby had me do. That was my first real experience with the Bible, and it's been a life changer for me."

So it was agreed that the book-group-turned-angels-group would now become the angels' Bible study book group. In the coming year, they would take turns selecting small portions of Scripture, which they would read at home and then discuss together.

With much still to do for Christmas, it was time to part ways. As the women exchanged warm hugs and kind words, in heaven above, a smiling Abby Wentworth gazed down upon the four Christmas angels . . .

And winked.

Melody Carlson is the award-winning author of over two hundred books, including *Christmas at Harrington's*, *The Christmas Pony*, *A Simple Christmas Wish*, *The Christmas Cat*, and *The Christmas Joy Ride*. Melody has received a *Romantic Times* Career Achievement Award in the inspirational market for her books. She and her husband live in central Oregon. For more information about Melody, visit her website at www.melody carlson.com.

Meet Melody at
MelodyCarlson.com

- Enter a contest for a signed book
- Read her monthly newsletter
- Find a special page for book clubs
- Discover more books by Melody

Become a fan on Facebook
Melody Carlson Books

WANT MORE CHRISTMAS?
Catch these eBooks!

Melody Carlson creates wonderful Christmas stories that make you want to curl up to a fireplace and get lost in a good story.